T0129056

Also written by Barbara Nattress:

Dreams in the Mist
Loyalist House Season I

HANNAH'S SEARCH

Loyalist House, Bed and Breakfast

Barbara Nattress

Order this book online at www.trafford.com
or email orders@trafford.com

Most Trafford titles are also available at major online book retailers.

Printed in the United States of America.

ISBN: 978-1-4907-3603-7 (sc)
ISBN: 978-1-4907-3602-0 (hc)
ISBN: 978-1-4907-3601-3 (e)

Library of Congress Control Number: 2014908719

Trafford rev. 05/13/2014

 www.trafford.com

North America & international
toll-free: 1 888 232 4444 (USA & Canada)
fax: 812 355 4082

AUTHOR'S NOTES

Hannah's Search is the sequel to *Dreams in the Mist* and continues the story of the relationship between Marilee, the present owner of Loyalist House, and the resident ghost, Hannah. As an author, I thought *Dreams in the Mist* would be a stand-alone book. But many of my friends and readers told me I could not leave Hannah and Peter separated as I did at the end of Season I. I have continued their story and once again used the members of the Van Every family as characters living in the desperate times of hardship during the War of 1812.

As this is a fictional story, I have taken liberties with assigning names to characters, and I apologize to any members of my family who know the real story.

I have tried to keep the historical aspects true especially in relationship to dates and events that took place during the War of 1812.

ACKNOWLEDGMENTS

I would like to thank all my friends who encouraged me to keep writing to finish the story. Whenever I was out walking or at the grocery store, I seemed to meet friends who would ask why I was not home writing. Thank you for the encouragement.

I would also like to thank the staff at Country Heritage Park for giving me the opportunity to interpret the realities of pioneer life to elementary students. I certainly learned a lot about the basic equipment used on a pioneer farm.

Thank you, as well, to my sister-in-law Lynda for reading the first draft in installments and providing feedback.

A special thank-you to Michael Pilliteri at Riverview Cellars Estate Winery, Niagara on the Lake, Ontario for his help with the facts about operating a winery.

I hope you enjoy the continuing story of the young lovers torn apart by war and loyalties.

JUNE

Hannah was very confused. Why did she have bits of weeds stuck in her hair and on her clothing? Why was her dress so wrinkled and dirty? Why was she in the attic by herself, and although it was dark outside, why could she see everything in the room so well? She suddenly remembered the letters Peter had written to her and wondered if they might tell her when she was to meet him. He must be waiting for her at the river by now, and she needed to confirm the time he wrote in the last letter.

"That's why I am in the attic so I can get the letters I hid in my doll," she said to herself. Under the window was the trunk where the doll was hidden, so Hannah walked across the room to the trunk, but as she passed the window, lights by the river caught her eye. She could see soldiers moving around on the dock and holding lanterns over the water and near the bushes as if looking for something. She really hoped Peter was safe and not hiding in their favorite spot.

Hannah continued to watch the events unfold by the water but was puzzled as to why her parents were with the soldiers. Suddenly someone was reaching in the water, and a large object was pulled out near the bushes along the shore. Hannah held her breath, hoping it was not Peter and then noticed the clothing was that of a woman. It was a dark-colored dress with a dark shawl wrapped around the body.

It seemed odd that a few minutes ago it was dark outside, but now it was daylight, and the shore was clearly visible. Time was not making any sense. Hannah knew she must find the letters and read them again, but she was mesmerized by the activity at the river. She saw her mother with a look of horror on her face and almost collapse in grief. Her father had tears streaming down his expressionless face as he held Mrs. Van Every. Hannah then looked once again at the body pulled from the river and recognized the dress, the shawl, and the face.

"No," she moaned and began to sob loudly. "That's me they are lifting out of the river," she sobbed. "Why has this happened?" As she put her hands to her neck, she felt several holes in the skin. "I'm dead," she said.

Hannah began to remember the events that evening by the river and now realized she had been shot by the soldiers while waiting to meet Peter at their favorite spot. She would never talk to him again or touch him or marry him as they had planned. Who would tell Peter she was dead? Hannah sat on the trunk by the window watching the group carry her body to the house.

"I must stay here and watch for Peter as he must be near. I will stay here forever to watch for him," she sobbed.

*　　*　　*

Marilee sat bolt upright in bed. The sobbing had begun again, only now it seemed more intense and sadder than before. This was the third night in a row she had been awakened by the noises in the attic. For several weeks, the noises had been silent; but suddenly, they had returned. During the last year, they had been sporadic and irregular; but for the past three nights, Marilee heard the sobbing. Sometimes it was so loud Marilee was sure the guests in the house would hear it, and she would have to explain the noises at breakfast.

She and Phillip had decided that if guests heard strange noises and inquired about them, they would explain the story of Hannah and Peter rather than hide it. After researching the family history of the house, Marilee and Phillip had put together a story of the young lovers and their dreams and how, because of a war, they were never to be realized.

Marilee looked at the clock, and it was almost six, so she decided to get up. They had three rooms filled this week for all five days, so things were busy at the B&B. By the weekend, all five rooms at Loyalist House would be occupied. The season was well under way, and Loyalist House was quickly filling up well in advance. There were several weeks in July and August that were fully booked.

Marilee had decided that to properly serve their guests this year she would need help with the cleaning and the cooking and had been fortunate enough to find a true gem of a person. Julie had started working at Loyalist House just this month and was proving to be invaluable. Marilee was happy to relinquish some of the responsibility and was thrilled that Julie was such a good cook. This morning was no exception. When Marilee entered the kitchen, Julie was already preparing scones and muffins.

"We will likely be explaining the lover's story again this morning," Marilee told Julie. "The sobbing was really loud last night, and I'm sure the guests must have heard. I'm not sure why this has started again and why it is so intense this time. We may have to go to the attic just to check out if anything has changed up there."

"I'll go, but only if someone is with me," said Julie. Julie's eyes were as big as saucers, and her voice was quite soft as though she didn't want anyone to hear what she was saying. "I'm not sure we should disturb the ghost if she is unhappy as we don't want her to become angry."

Marilee and Phillip had originally decided to hire a person to encourage the ghost to leave the house, a ghost buster of sorts. In fact, Marilee, along with her friend Jeannie, had booked a man named Manfred to come in September to exorcize the ghost from the house. After much discussion, they were all beginning to have second thoughts and were waiting until September to make the decision. "Manfred will be back from his trip by then," Phillip had commented earlier, "and he might even have some ideas on how to appease the ghost."

Marilee agreed, "Especially since we think we know who the ghost is now."

Julie had been told the story when she came to work at the house as Marilee wanted to be sure she was fine about a ghost being present while she carried on her work throughout the house.

"How are you going to find out more about Peter and if he returned?" asked Julie as she took the first batch of muffins from the oven.

Marilee was silent for a moment as she thought about the huge task ahead of her. "I guess I will have to research all the property deeds around here during that time period to see if Peter's name appears on any of them. Marriage licenses may also help if any can be found. Since the town was burned in 1813, it may be hard to find anything that old."

The back door opened, and Phillip came into the kitchen. He had been up very early to be ready for deliveries of supplies for the new winery across the road. The purchase of twenty acres across from the B&B had closed, and Loyalist House Winery was now an official winery in the area.

Over half the property was planted in several varieties of grapes, and the rest was a combination of grassland and fruit trees. It had once been a farm with animals and crops and had belonged to a family that had come to the area to escape persecution during the Revolutionary War. The farm had changed owners and uses a number of times, but there was one original brick building still on the property that was in fairly good shape.

Phillip and his partners Dave and Mike had decided to restore the original building and add onto it to create the public spaces for the winery. They were also building spaces to make the wine, store it and all the equipment needed to run a winery. It was a large project, but the three partners were enthusiastic and anxious to begin producing wine.

Phillip looked at Marilee and Julie and said, "Who's going to tell the guests the story about the noises this morning?" It had become a game of sorts as to who would get to tell the story of Peter and Hannah when guests revealed they heard noises in the night. "I did it last week, and I have to meet with some people later this morning, so one of you can have the honor today," he stated as he headed to his office upstairs. Even with his new adventure, Phillip still enjoyed interacting with the guests and telling them of all the tourist opportunities in the area. Now that his passion for wine was increased tenfold, he loved talking to the guests at happy hour, especially about wine.

Julie looked at Marilee and said, "You can tell them today. I still feel a bit odd talking about Hannah as if she wasn't here. I always worry she can hear me and might take offense to something I say. It's just such a sad story that I always worry I may break down and cry as I'm telling it. We don't want to make our guests sad after all, and we don't want them to worry either."

"I will be happy to tell them. I have almost memorized the story by now," Marilee said as she finished alternating strawberries with yogurt in the parfait glasses. "If they ask you, just say you have to finish something in the kitchen and you'll be back and then come and get me."

"Thanks Marilee, you always save me. Now I have to go in and make sure the table is perfect as the guests will be down shortly." Julie continued into the dining room and completed the finishing touches on the table. As usual, the flowers were fresh and seasonal, and the silver and glassware were shiny and sparkling. Once again, breakfast was ready for the guests at Loyalist House.

It always took about ten minutes before all the guests arrived for breakfast so Julie and Marilee were kept busy serving juice and coffee. Once everyone was down, Marilee began to serve the fruit course.

"Did anyone hear crying in the night?" asked the guest at the head of the table. There were looks of embarrassment as no one seemed to want to pry into the others' private lives, but one other guest quietly said she thought she heard something.

Marilee decided this was her cue to jump in and explain. "You may or may not know, but we have a resident spirit here at Loyalist House. Part of this house was built around 1800, and the family lived here for almost thirty years.

During the War of 1812, one of the daughters, probably about fourteen, was killed by British soldiers down by the river. She had been in love with a neighbor boy and was secretly engaged to him. When his parents decided to side with the Americans and move across the river, the lovers continued to meet along the shore at night.

At one of these planned meetings, soldiers were patrolling the river; and when they saw some movement on the shore, the soldiers fired shots. Hannah Van Every was shot, and we think she remains in the attic watching for her beloved Peter. We know all this from letters we found in a trunk and from records of residents who lived in the area during that period.

Hannah is a sad spirit but has never caused any trouble and can only be heard sobbing or moving the trunk that contains her doll. There is really is no need to be concerned as she stays in the attic."

Before the guests could ask any questions, Marilee left the dining room to begin serving the rest of the breakfast. She smiled at Julie as she entered the kitchen and whispered, "Now come all the questions." It was always the same, and the questions were almost always the same, even though the guests changed.

When Marilee reentered the dining room carrying the French toast, the questions began. Mr. Johnson, at the end of the table, asked, "Has anything destructive ever been done to the house?"

Marilee assured him, "No, only the trunk seems to get moved in the attic from one side over to the window. We think Hannah sits on it and watches out the window for Peter."

Mrs. Johnson asked, "Did Peter and his family ever return to the area, and how did Hannah's parents handle her death?"

Marilee said, "We don't know for sure, but we think he may have. We are doing more research to try and find out if he ever returned and lived in the area." The questions always took the same path. The men always asked about any destructive activity by the ghost, and the women were always concerned about the people related to Hannah and how they coped with her loss.

Marilee continued, "I'm sure her parents and the rest of her family were not only devastated but also afraid. The British would have been watching their land for the appearance of other Americans crossing the river possibly as spies. The war was really heating up at that point, and within a few weeks of Hannah's death, war was declared, and major battles were fought in the area."

Marilee excused herself from the dining room and returned to the kitchen to continue breakfast preparations. It would have been easy to be drawn into a lengthy discussion on the history of the area, but she knew she had food that might burn if not attended to immediately.

Breakfast continued on with no further questions, and the guests departed for various tourist activities for the day. Today, Marilee was looking forward to going to the museum to continue her research on war activities as well as finding out more about Peter. "But first I must clean up the rooms," she said and then realized she was talking to herself. Marilee picked up the phone and dialed a number she obviously called a lot. "Hi Jeannie, how are you?"

"Great," said Jeannie. "What are you up to today?"

Marilee felt she must be reading her mind. "I'm going to the museum to find out more about Peter. I want to know when he came back to this side of the river. The sobbing is still going on in the attic, so I need to find out more to help understand all this. Do you want to come with me?"

"Of course I do," replied Jeannie. "I wouldn't miss it."

Being Marilee's neighbor, Jeannie was involved in most of the history discoveries with Marilee. Together they had discovered the original owners of Loyalist House, and that it was the daughter Hannah whose spirit now inhabited the attic. Being a long-term resident, Jeannie had many friends in town which opened up a lot of doors when you needed to find out information.

"Come over at eleven, and we'll go to the museum and then have lunch," said Marilee.

"See you later," said Jeannie. And she hung up.

Phillip walked in the back door and asked, "Marilee do you have time for coffee? I need to bring you up to date on the winery happenings."

"Not really, but sit here and have coffee and talk to me while I do up these dishes," said Marilee. "I hope it's good news and doesn't involve a ton of money."

Phillip poured his coffee and began to tell Marilee the latest news about the winery. Marilee knew the property was twenty acres just across the road from the B&B and that most of it had vines already growing. She knew his partners Mike and Dave wanted to replant some of the vines and add some more as well.

Phillip continued, "Mike and Dave have had the plans for the buildings drawn up, and we want you to see them and tell us if the tasting and boutique space is right. We want to apply for the permits by the end of the month so we can get started with building. We won't be ready for customers in the new building until next summer, but that's OK as we can still produce wine at the bottling facility where the past owners made wine."

"When do you think you might be planting the new vines?" asked Marilee.

"Either in the late summer or fall, but they won't really produce for several years," Phillip answered.

"What will happen to the old barn that is on the property?" Marilee interrupted.

Phillip continued, "We have to decide the varieties we want to promote and then decide what to plant. As for the barn, we think we might be able to save most of it and utilize it in some way for the public space. We have to have an architect look at it from a safety aspect before we make any decisions."

"It's just in such a good location and could be so attractive from the road," Marilee said. "It might really draw people into the winery."

"Good point," said Phillip. "That would be a draw for the winery. We'll keep that in mind." Let's set a time at the end of this week to meet with Dave and Mike so we can look at the plans. How about Friday at five?"

"We have guests arriving that evening, but we could meet in the kitchen here so we can hear when people arrive," Marilee added.

Marilee finished up the dishes, while Phillip finished his coffee and scone. Both had plans for today but agreed to meet on the patio at five for wine and cheese with some of their guests.

It wasn't long before Jeannie arrived, and the two women drove together to the museum. As always, the conversation turned to Hannah and her latest escapades in the attic.

"Last night, the noises were even louder and longer than before," said Marilee. "I'm not sure what we are going to do. I know it would be so mean to try and get rid of her, and that may not even work. Maybe if we can find out more information about Peter, it will help us figure out what to do. I think some of the guests were really disturbed last night with the crying. They may have thought it was another guest rather than a ghost."

"I agree that getting rid of Hannah may not be the answer," added Jeannie. "But if you try to keep her as an attraction, you may lose some guests. Have you put the letters back in the doll yet?"

"No, not yet. I can't decide whether to use the originals or the copies. Do ghosts notice things like that?" asked Marilee.

"I have no idea," said Jeannie. "But I think you should return the originals, just in case."

Marilee changed the subject and said, "Today, we need to try and find out when Peter came back to this area and where he stayed. We know he might not have been welcome since his family basically traded sides. I guess we could start with looking at the land ownership to see what happened to their land after they crossed the river to side with the Americans."

"Good idea," said Jeannie. "Who do you suppose ran the farm while they were gone? Would the local government take away land when a farmer deserted?"

"All good questions to which I have no answers," remarked Marilee.

They reached the museum parking lot and walked to the museum in silence, each with their own thoughts about where to start and with hopes of finding answers. Once inside, as always, they met a number of friends and chatter about local news took precedence over work. Everyone in town seemed to know about the ghost at Loyalist House, so the question of what Hannah was up to always was part of the conversation.

Marilee explained, "We are here today to find out what happened to Peter so maybe we can solve the mystery and help Hannah out of her misery, though heaven knows I have no idea how to do that." She was hoping someone there might have an idea of where to start or know someone who might enlighten them. It was not to be though as no one knew about the Gillham family or what happened to their land.

Marilee and Jeannie went to the files of land ownership and began their search. It was very quiet in the room, and for about fifteen minutes, no one spoke.

"Well, look at this," whispered Jeannie as though she was afraid someone might hear her. "I may have found the beginning of an answer."

Marilee jumped from her chair and ran over to where Jeannie was working. "What did you find?" she asked.

"It seems that during the war after Peter's family had moved across the river, a farmworker took care of the land. He was employed by Mr. Gillham and had apparently come there with the Gillhams when they arrived as Loyalists during the American Revolution. There are rumors that he may have been a slave while they lived in New York area, but when they came here, he was granted his freedom but continued to stay and work for the Gillhams," Jeannie read.

"Wow" was all Marilee could say. "Where did you find that article?"

"It's an article on slavery and the Blacks in this area," said Jeannie. "It's quite interesting about how they were treated in this area, just the opposite of their treatment farther south. We might want to read the whole book written about the Blacks in Niagara," suggested Jeannie.

"Let's see if we can check that out before we leave. What was the farmworker's name?" asked Marilee. "Was it Joseph by any chance?"

"No. It was Eli," answered Jeannie.

"I was hoping you would find a black man named Joseph. Don't you remember the farmworker who delivered letters between Hannah and Peter? His name was Joseph," said Marilee. "He may have stayed behind to keep the Van Every farm running, and he did know all the workings of the farm so he would be the logical one."

Even though it wasn't the name they had hoped for, they were both excited about this bit of information and decided to look further through these records another day. They went back to the front desk to inquire about borrowing the book, and after checking it out, they walked to the bakery-coffee shop to plot their next move over coffee and biscotti. Biscotti always helped with decisions, and it didn't hurt that Have Another Cookie had at least ten varieties.

Marilee started asking Jeannie what she had found in the article at the museum. "What did they say about slaves in this area, and did they mention Eli or a Joseph by name? Where did they work, and for how long?" Marilee fired off questions so fast that Jeannie couldn't get a word in edgewise.

"Hold on, speak slower. I can't even remember the first question you are going so fast," said Jeannie. "First of all, it did say that there was a fairly large Black population in this area as many Loyalists brought their slaves with them when they escaped from the U.S. during the Revolutionary War. Apparently, Governor Simcoe had declared that all slaves were free once they came to the area. Even at that, most stayed with their owners and worked as farmhands helping develop the property and plant the crops. It did mention a Joseph but did not give his last name. He apparently came with a family from New York and stayed with them. It did say he worked for several farmers in the area and eventually stayed in Niagara and lived here until he died in 1857. He even owned property in the town later on."

Marilee was very excited. "Wouldn't it be fantastic if that was the same Joseph that delivered notes for Hannah and Peter?" said Marilee. "If he owned property, we must be able to find out his last name especially if it was after 1813. I thought in the letters it said he worked for the Van Every family but knew Peter's father."

Jennie speculated out loud, "I guess the people in this town must have been quite tolerant after all they had been through during the Revolution." Then she added, "We need to go back to the museum and the library to get more material on the Black community. If it really is the same Joseph, this might help us find out what we need to know about Peter. Let's meet at the museum tomorrow at one to see what we can find. Does that work for you?"

"Sounds good," said Marilee. "We have no one coming in tomorrow, so it's an easy day."

The ride home was silent as they were both deep in thought about the information they had discovered today and about what they hoped to find out tomorrow. Marilee dropped Jeannie off at her house and continued home. She noticed several guests cars were back in the driveway, so some may have returned for the day. She would get the wine and nibblies ready for happy hour and join the guests on the patio.

Tonight, Phillip was introducing a new Riesling to the guests, and Marilee had put together a platter with almonds, havarti cheese, green apple slices, and a pesto cream cheese dip. In a basket, she put toasted slices of French bread.

The mood on the patio was quite happy when she arrived with the food. Phillip was already there pouring wine and relating facts of wineries and wines in the area. There was a slight breeze and the perfume from the peonies, and some late lilacs was drifting across the patio. This really was an ideal spot to sit with a glass of wine at this time of day. The conversation continued for a while, and then the guests left to get ready for the evening.

Phillip and Marilee stayed on the patio for a while discussing their day before going in to start dinner. "We may have found out who was running the Gillham's farm during the war," said Marilee. "It looks like it may have been a farmhand who may have previously been a slave." She continued to relate some of the information they had found about the Black community in the area.

Phillip was intrigued as he was currently reading a book about slaves coming north through various ways. "Many were trying to escape from terrible conditions and masters so used secret and interesting ways to hide and be smuggled into this country," added Phillip. "Wouldn't it be a coincidence if Joseph had come by the underground railway? The dates may be wrong, but as soon as news of abolition traveled to the south where there was still slavery, there was a steady stream of men, women, and children trying to find ways to come here. There's another avenue for you to explore to solve this mystery," he said as he gathered up the dishes to take inside.

The rest of the evening disappeared, taking care of dinner and preparations for tomorrow's breakfast, and before they knew it, the clock stuck eleven. Marilee casually added, "I hope there is no noise tonight as I am very tired and the guests might be also."

*   *   *

Peter had watched from the riverbank as the British soldiers first fired their guns and then inspected something on the shore at the Van Every property. It was dark, so he hadn't been able to tell what was happening. He just hoped it did not involve Hannah, and the soldiers had not caught her down by the dock. When they disappeared up the bank, he quickly returned to the other side of the river. He stayed awake all night, and as soon as it was light, he returned and watched safely from the other side. From behind the bushes, he saw not only the soldiers but also Mr. and Mrs. Van Every following them to the water's edge. He feared the worst, and when he saw something being lifted from the water and Mrs. Van Every crouching over the body and being comforted, he knew it was Hannah they had pulled from the water. "It was my fault," he whispered to himself. "I should never have agreed to meet her at the river. Now what will I do? If I go back, they will hate me, and I may be considered a traitor. I can't stay here as I will never be happy on this side of the river. Why did my parents make the decision to leave, and why did I have to come with them?"

Peter knew some of these answers but was so engulfed with grief over the loss of his beloved Hannah he did not know how he was going to survive. He slowly returned up the riverbank to his new home not knowing how he would hide his misery from his family. He couldn't tell them the whole story as his father would be furious for taking chances, both with his life and Hannah's and her family.

For several days, he kept to himself as much as he could and only went to the house to eat and sleep. He kept himself busy with chores around the farm all the while thinking about how he could somehow return to Upper Canada without going to jail.

Later that week, his father asked him to go to the nearest settlement with him to pick up some supplies for a new building. Peter really didn't want to go but after was glad he had. The trading post was near the docks, and while there, he heard many of the men talking about the war. The word was that it was imminent, and anyone old enough to shoot a gun would be requested to fight. He also overheard some men talking about crossing the river to the other side and not fighting for the Americans. Apparently, there was a camp near the fort where they could easily blend in and not be branded as traitors.

Peter listened carefully to the details they were discussing, and because he looked too young to be a threat, no one seemed to notice his presence. On the way back to the farm with the supplies,

Peter decided to ask his father about the farm they had left in Upper Canada.

"I could not sell the farm as neighbors may have suspected we would go across the river, and we would have been labelled traitors," said Mr. Gillham. "I still have the deed to the land but have left it with our farmhand Eli. Someday when all this war nonsense is over, we may decide to return."

Peter was astounded. He really wanted to ask his father to allow him to return and run the farm, but Peter knew he would never agree. Was all this moving and now Hannah's death really necessary?

Peter began to formulate a plan in his mind. It would be dangerous, but he had to do it. He decided to leave within the week. The weather was warm, and the days were long so he could travel later to reach his destination. He hadn't figured out how he would get across the river as he had no money, but surely he would find a way once he was at the landing. He would return to Upper Canada.

*   *   *

The rest of the week was relatively quiet in the attic, so the guests slept well, ate well, and enjoyed their visit at Loyalist House. Marilee did hear sobbing several nights, but the intensity had lessened, so the guests probably had not heard it. That was the one great advantage of this house. Most of the guest rooms were farther from the original part of the house where the attic was located.

Friday was an easy day for breakfast, and there were only three of the five rooms to get ready for weekend guests. This would be a busy weekend though as it was one of the summer fruit festivals sponsored by a local church. Phillip reminded Marilee at breakfast of their meeting with his partners at five, so she planned her day accordingly. She was able to be ready for the next wave of guests by mid afternoon and actually had time to sit down and organize some of her findings about Peter so she could plan her next move. By five, she was already sitting on the patio with wine and snacks when Phillip and his partners arrived.

Immediately, Dave asked, "What have you found out about the young lovers this week? Julie told me about the loud noises waking the guests." Julie was Dave's sister-in-law, so he had heard the story from family.

Marilee at first was startled; hoping the story was not all over town and relieved to find out it came from Julie. "We still are no farther ahead in finding out information about Hannah's lover, but at least we have a few more leads to follow," she said. Marilee then gave a short recant of the events they did know as Mike was not aware of the story.

"Hopefully we won't find another ghost in the barn when we go to fix it up," added Dave. "We do have to do an archaeological dig before we can start anything. What do you suppose that will turn up?"

The conversation then turned to the winery and its development. Mike, who was the specialist in the crop area, explained which vines were needed to produce specific wines and how many of each per acre would ensure them an adequate amount of grapes for production. This of course was based on perfect weather and growing conditions. The planting schedule was scheduled for late summer and the following spring. As there was no permit required for this part of the development, it could be scheduled well in advance.

Marilee was curious about the dig required and asked, "When will the dig take place, and who does these things? What are they hoping to find, and what happens if they do find anything significant?"

Dave replied, "There are companies who specialize in this and often work only in one area where they are familiar with the history. They can't start the dig until after we have the building permit, so we are in a holding pattern right now. Usually, what they find are pieces of crockery from households and buttons from clothing. We have to hope they find nothing historically or ecologically significant, or our time line could be seriously delayed."

"First, though, let's look at the drawings of what the public spaces might look like, and if we all agree, we can submit these to the town for a building permit subject of course to an uneventful dig," said Phillip.

The next half hour was spent discussing the size and shape of rooms and all the other design elements involved in having an aesthetic and functional boutique winery. Amazingly, they all agreed on the architectural plans with no changes, so Monday morning, these plans would be delivered to the town offices for approval. This was the first big hurdle to cross off their list, but there were still lots more to go. The conversation continued until the doorbell rang signaling the arrival of guests for the weekend.

Marilee answered the door and found four of the five groups waiting to enter. She was quite surprised and even more so when she discovered they all knew one another. The fifth couple were arriving later as their drive from home was longer.

The lobby of Loyalist House was quite large, but with eight guests and twice as much luggage, the area became very congested. Marilee decided to take them to their rooms first and then have them fill in their registration. Phillip arrived to help get all the luggage to the rooms, and twenty minutes later, Marilee and Phillip had five registration forms waiting for all the guests to fill in.

All had been invited to the patio for wine and cheese, so registering might seem less formal while sipping wine and chatting. The last couple arrived and were dispatched to their room, and Phillip and Marilee quickly began getting the nibbles ready for happy hour.

Once on the patio and with registration completed, the relaxing began. This group apparently had been friends in college and had stayed in touch for over twenty years. Every year, they met at a new location and enjoyed a weekend exploring, eating, and partying. This year, Loyalist House was their choice. The question began immediately about the best winery, best restaurant, and best tourist attraction in the area. Phillip was in his element now. He explained about the number of wineries in the area, and the group were both surprised and delighted.

"And next year, there will be a new one right here at Loyalist House for you to visit," added Phillip. "We are starting a new winery and hope to have it up and running within the year. We do have some wine bottled from this past year, but we will be buying grapes from other farmers in the area until we have enough of our own grapes to be self-sufficient. Tonight, I am serving you one of our own wines. It is a pinot noir and was bottled two years ago. Marilee, what food have you paired with it tonight?"

Marilee explained the food on the platter. "I have included some goat cheese which is local, walnuts, and fresh strawberries for tasting with the wine. I have also baked some mushroom caps containing chopped mushroom stems, bread crumbs, onions, and a pinch of cinnamon. It is all blended together with a bit of cream cheese. I think you will enjoy the combination of flavors with the pinot."

One of the couples, Joe and Corrie, lived near the wine trail in the southwest part of the province and knew a bit about wine production. Coming right to the point, Joe asked, "How much does it cost to set up a self-sufficient winery in this area?"

Phillip wasn't willing to divulge his exact budget but stated, "A lot of money which is why I have two partners with deep pockets. It really depends on the price of the land and how big you want to go, so it's hard to give an exact figure."

The conversation continued and touched on everything from would they bottle their own wine to whether corks were better than screw top lids. There was never a lull in the conversation until someone noticed it was almost seven, and the group had reservations for dinner that evening. They quickly thanked their host and hostess and left to get ready for dinner.

Before leaving, two of the wives, Linda and Sue, asked if they could serve birthday cake later in the lounge as it was Randy's birthday, and they had brought a cake with them. Marilee quickly went into planning mode and offered to keep the cake in the kitchen and have coffee and tea ready to serve when they returned.

The plans were made, and Sue said, "Thank you so much, and you and Phillip must join us for the celebration."

Marilee waited while Sue brought the cake down and then returned to the kitchen. Turning to Phillip, she said, "I think you may need to have either some scotch or beer on hand for later as this party may not end tonight with just tea and coffee."

Phillip agreed but said, "Right now, I need supper, so I am going to grill a couple of those small steaks we bought the other day. You fix a salad, and that will make a great dinner."

Dinner on the patio was perfect as the weather was warm, and the scent of roses settled over the patio. After dinner, some prep work for breakfast kept Marilee busy; and just as she was about to sit down, the group returned, ready to celebrate.

It was a very warm evening for mid-June, so Marilee suggested they have the birthday party on the patio. Everyone agreed and was soon settled at the table. Two of the men, Doug and Bruce, were carrying a small bag with them which soon revealed an unopened bottle of twenty-year-old single malt scotch.

Phillip acknowledged it as he arrived with a tray of glasses. "It looks like we are on the same wavelength here. I figured we should have more than coffee to toast the birthday boy. I also have some interesting red wine you might like to taste as well." He then returned to the kitchen to bring the wine for tasting.

The party was quite proper at first as everyone sang "Happy Birthday" and ate cake, drank coffee, and chatted about past birthdays and special parties. Then Phillip began the wine tasting. When the wine was done, they started on the scotch.

The stories about good times became funnier and the voices louder. Marilee was hoping parties like this would not disturb the neighbors or their resident spirit.

It was well past midnight when several of the women suggested they call it a night, or no one would want to explore the next day. Marilee suggested they have breakfast at eight thirty or nine instead of eight, and everyone agreed on nine. She also hoped that if Hannah decided to go on a crying spree tonight, everyone would be so deep in sleep they would not hear her.

*　　*　　*

Hannah had been watching for days but had not seen Peter anywhere. She had also discovered that she could leave the attic and visit other parts of the house. At first, it was too sad as she seemed to always find her mother crying. Her younger sister never went outside, and her father and brother spent all their time doing chores around the farm. Her family seemed to be falling apart, and it was all her fault for being at the river. They didn't seem to spend much time talking to each other anymore. Hannah felt better going downstairs at night after everyone had gone to bed as that way she could see things she remembered, but it made her feel even sadder as she couldn't be a part of those things anymore.

One evening, she traveled down to the kitchen and was surprised to find her parents sitting at the table talking. The look on their faces was very serious.

Mr. Van Every stated, "We must be ready to flee at any time. Pack a small case with something warm for the children and yourself and have bread ready to put in it as well. We will have to walk over land to the west to my brother's place away from the river. It will take at least a day, maybe two, so we will have to be prepared to sleep in the woods. The soldiers could take over our house and land as the point of land down by the river is an advantage to the British. They can see both ways along the river."

"Will you be coming with us?" asked Mrs. Van Every.

"Not likely as the army may make me fight with them or be considered a traitor," said Hannah's father. "Young William will go with you, and he knows how to use a gun."

Hannah was horrified. Even though she could not talk to them, she did not want them to leave her or the house. Why were they making these plans now? What had happened to make them decide this? She then heard someone at the door. Both her parents were silent until a voice identified themselves as one of the farmhands.

Mr. Van Every then explained to the man, who was the farm manager, that the war was intensifying, and troops may come and take over the farm because of its vantage point on the river. If that happened, he and the other workers would be free to go wherever they would be safe. He told him where the family would be going, and there was probably a safe spot for the workers at his brothers as well. He then walked outside with the worker and gave further instructions regarding animals on the farm, shook his hand, and wished him safe journeys during these terrible times.

Hannah returned back to the attic and sat by the window watching the river. All this trouble and war was more than she could comprehend. She began to sob, loud long sobs that lasted until daybreak.

*   *   *

JULY

By July, the gardens looked wonderful, there had been enough rain to keep everything lush, and a deep green color and the fragrant flowers were so abundant that bouquets for inside the house could be picked daily. Marilee enjoyed having fresh flowers inside Loyalist House and was proud that they all came from planning which flowers to plant and hard work. Of course, many of the plants had been there when she and Phillip purchased the property, but their care had kept them strong.

Today's arrangements were composed of roses and lavender with some greens, daisies, fern, and hosta leaves and a variety of colorful annuals that had been planted in May. For interest's sake, Marilee had included some basil stems.

Today, there were five couples arriving for the weekend, so things at the B&B would be busy. In fact, the whole month was almost booked solid. This weekend, there were a number of 1812 commemorative activities taking place as well as all the annual events. It was indeed a busy weekend. Marilee and Jeannie were involved at the Museum and in the walking tours around town showcasing the historic homes.

Marilee and Julie were just finishing up the food preparations for the next morning when Phillip arrived in the kitchen with two bottles of wine.

"We must taste these, and I need your opinion on both bottles," he said as he reached for some wine glasses. "This is the batch from two years ago and is about to be bottled for release. One is a cabernet franc and the other a merlot. They are from one of the vineyards out along the lakeshore, and since that year had such a good growing season, I think they should be outstanding."

"We will be out in ten minutes," said Marilee. "Phillip gets so excited about a new bottle of wine I can't even imagine what he's going to be like when the winery opens."

"He is passionate about it," replied Julie. "Go ahead and join him, and I'll finish up here and be out when I'm done. I always think it is fun to taste the new batch as well, but that's probably been ingrained into me due to family interest."

Marilee added, "I can't believe Dave and Mike aren't here as well, especially Dave, since he is the winemaker. I'll meet you outside. Just leave the rest of those dishes, and I'll do them at supper time."

Phillip, Dave, and Mike were sitting on the patio ready to taste. They had opened the bottle to let it breathe and were waiting for the girls to come out and join them.

"Aha. The three musketeers are together for this momentous occasion. I was surprised not to see you when Phillip came to show us," said Marilee.

"We would never miss a chance to taste the best wine ever produced," said Mike.

Julie came out the back door, and Phillip felt the wine was ready to pour. He poured a taste in everyone's glass and offered a toast. "Here's to 2011 wine and to Loyalist House Winery."

Glasses were clinked, and all repeated the toast. It was very quiet for a few minutes while each tasted and analyzed the product. There was sniffing, glass swirling, sucking through teeth, and swallowing. A second taste was taken, and the process repeated.

Finally, Phillip spoke, "I have to say that's pretty good wine."

"And it will only get better with age," added Dave.

They all agreed the merlot was going to be a winner. The same process was repeated for the cabernet franc, but there was not quite as much enthusiasm for the result. They would let it sit for a while longer and see if the aging process might improve it. They were a happy group though and continued tasting until the bottle was empty. It was decided the merlot would be sent to be bottled next week, and the other would remain in the casks for another two months.

"We shall meet again right here in two months to retaste the cabernet franc," said Dave. "We do have four more barrels of 2011 wines to decide about, so I guess this little meeting better happen twice next week."

"Set it all up for Wednesday night, same time, same place," Mike added while looking at Marilee for her approval.

"Fine with me," she said.

With that, the group left the patio, and Phillip and Marilee went inside to begin dinner and wait for the guests to arrive. As usual, just as they were ready to sit down to dinner, the doorbell rang, signaling guests' arrival. This seemed to happen all the time, leading Phillip to believe they were not meant to eat a hot dinner.

While the first set of guests were registering, the next ones arrived; and within twenty minutes, all five couples were welcomed to Loyalist House for the weekend.

Tonight, there would be no happy hour, but Phillip made sure to invite everyone to the patio for drinks the next night. One of the guests remarked that the testimonials on their website raved about the hospitality shown at Loyalist House, especially the enjoyment of the happy hour on the patio.

"In fact," he replied, "that is why we booked here."

The couples all dispersed to their rooms and prepared to go out for dinner, so Phillip and Marilee returned to the kitchen and heated their dinner and started again.

The rest of the evening was quiet. Marilee had all the preparations for breakfast done before eight o'clock, so she decided to begin reading the book she borrowed from the library about the Black population in the area during the war years. It was easy to read, and she could envision the areas talked about by the descriptions of the town told by the author. Some of these cottages were still standing and had been renovated to become lovely small weekend homes.

One by one, the couples returned; and by half past ten, all was quiet upstairs, and Marilee and Phillip decided to retire for the evening. As she did every night, Marilee recited her evening mantra. "Please let Hannah have a quiet and happy night tonight." Sometimes, it worked but not always.

Tonight would not be a quiet night.

*　　*　　*

Hannah was terribly anxious. She flitted about the house both day and night trying to keep a watch on her family. She saw her mother packing things in a small case and making those dry biscuits that she did not like, so she knew they were planning on leaving. One night while her family were all asleep, she crept into the room where the case was and unpacked all the things her mother had put in. The next morning, she saw her mother sigh and repack the clothes. When she looked closer, she noticed her mother had tears in her eyes. This made Hannah very sad, so she decided not to do that anymore.

On some of her day trips, Hannah was puzzled by what she saw. There were things happening in what she thought was their kitchen, but people dressed in odd garments were working at very strange pieces of equipment that she had never seen before. The odd thing about it was they were doing something with food that she recognized. It was as though she was drifting between two very different societies. One she had known and loved, and the other was beyond her imagination. The strangers never seemed to bother with her, except every once in a while someone would stop what they were doing and stare in her direction as though they had heard a noise.

Most of her nights though were spent at the window, watching the river for any sign of Peter. This is when emotions overcame her, and she sobbed beyond control. There was no one to comfort her or hold her and tell her things would be all right.

Hannah also did not understand why she was still here in the house. She always was told by her parents that when someone died, their soul went to heaven to live an everlasting life. This hardly seemed the life she was promised all those Sundays listening to the minister in church. There were times when small bits of doubt crept into her thoughts, and she began to think this might be another place. Maybe all the bad things she had done, especially sneaking out to see Peter, had given her a life in hell. This thought only made her sadder and want to continue the crying.

One evening as she sobbed and watched the river, she noticed a light and shadows moving along the bank. Her sobbing stopped.

"Maybe it was Peter. No, there were too many people," she said to herself. Now she began to worry about her family. The shadows became marching soldiers and proceeded up the path toward the house. "I must warn my family."

Hannah flew down through the floor and into the hall below and began to shriek as loud as she could. Back and forth along the hall, she floated, bumping into things she had not seen before and knocking jars attached to cords to the floor. She continued this until the room became very light and doors to several rooms opened.

"Oh, good," she thought. "My parents have heard me, and I have alerted them to the danger."

Suddenly, Hannah heard other screams; and when she looked again, she realized these were not her parents but strangers in her house. One man in baggy pants and a shirt was holding some kind of a stick.

"I must get out of here," she thought, and she disappeared through the wall at the end of the hall back to the attic.

*   *   *

Marilee and Phillip came running from the back of the house to the front upstairs hall in what must have been record time to find all five couples in a variety of night outfits standing in the hall. No one was screaming or speaking now, and two of the women looked quite pale.

"We saw a ghost in the hall," Mrs. Fenwick said in a shaky voice.

"Everyone, grab your housecoat and come down to the dining room," said Phillip.

Everyone did as they were told, and in a few minutes, all were seated at the dining room table. Marilee had gone to the kitchen to put the kettle on for tea, and Phillip had pulled out some bottles of whiskey and rye and glasses in case anyone needed something stronger. It seemed like the middle of the night but was only a bit after midnight.

Marilee then began the story of Hannah and all the events they knew about her. She also mentioned there were many anniversaries this year, of events that had happened during the War of 1812, and possibly Hannah was reliving some of them presently.

"This is the first time anyone has actually seen her in this part of the house," Marilee offered in hopes of reassuring everyone. "She usually stays in the attic and moves furniture and sobs. Once there has been a crisis, such as we just witnessed, it usually is quite calm for the rest of the night."

"I really think Marilee is right, and it has something to do with the timing and events of the war," added Phillip. "Now who would like a small drink before you go back to bed?"

Everyone had something, either tea or whiskey or both, and asked a lot of questions about the resident ghost. After about an hour of chatting and reassuring, everyone went back up to bed. The rest of the night remained quiet with no more apparitions sighted.

Breakfast the next morning was a lively affair. There were more questions about Hannah and about the war itself and how it had affected the area. As soon as the food had been served and the guests were enjoying that second cup of coffee, Marilee entered the dining room and sat on the bench by the window.

She began telling the group briefly about the whys and how the War of 1812 developed over the three years. "Fort George, located at the mouth of the Niagara River," began Marilee, "was a strategic location during the war and the site of several attacks by the Americans. At the end of May in 1813, a massive attack by the Americans was launched at the fort from the water. The battle lasted eight hours, and by that point, the fort was in ruins. The British had no choice but to withdraw and retreat to Burlington Heights at the end of the lake, leaving the fort, the town, and the surrounding area as occupied territory of the United States. American militia not only patrolled the streets and roads, they also took many men who had stayed behind, as prisoners. Houses and farms were pillaged and often occupied by soldiers during that time. Some of the local shopkeepers and farmers had joined the British Army but now had retreated, so women were either left to escape on their own, carry out the extra work of farming, or search the battlefields for loved ones in hopes of finding them alive."

Mrs. Fenwick asked, "Was this house used by soldiers during the war, and did the family survive except for Hannah?"

Marilee said, "The family, as far as we know, probably left during the occupation, and we think the farmhands helped keep the farm going. As this house was quite a distance from town, the prevalence of American soldiers was not as great. The area around this house was predominately British, and they were very protective, and they disliked the Americans as they had fled that country just thirty years earlier."

"Was this house ever burned?" asked another guest.

"Not that we know of," said Marilee. "It has had several additions, though, that were built well after the war and after the Van Everys sold the property." Marilee then continued to tell them about the reenactments taking place during the summer. "You may find American militia roaming the streets in town, and they may stop you and ask what your business is," she added. "It's all part of the celebrations this year." She then decided the history lesson had gone on long enough and offered the group some brochures describing events taking place in town this summer.

Everyone was excited about getting into town this morning to see what was going on. Just as plans were being discussed, Phillip strolled in and reminded them about the happy hour on the back patio tonight at five. The group was in high spirits as they left for the day, all looking forward to wine tasting and more discussions about the other kind of spirits.

At five, all the couples had returned from their sightseeing and theater encounters and were already sitting on the patio when Phillip and Marilee came out.

"Welcome," said Phillip. "I have a treat for you tonight. I have a 2010 merlot for you to taste tonight. It is from the bench area of Niagara and has beautiful plum overtones.

"And we are having baked brie with caramelized onions on top with just a sprinkling of rosemary. There are also some early plums straight from the farm," added Marilee. She always had freshly toasted slices of French bread on the platter as well.

The group enjoyed the wine and food, and soon it was gone, but the chatting continued for another hour when someone remembered the dinner reservations at seven.

July continued to be a busy month at the B&B. Guests arrived, enjoyed their stay, and many booked for the same time next year. Loyalist House was gaining popularity through word of mouth and through the Web site. Many guests wanted to book next year when the winery would have its grand opening in July.

There was still a lot of work left to do before that would happen. But today, there was good news. Phillip rushed into the house at noon calling Marilee as he rushed from room to room. Marilee was startled and thought for sure something dreadful had happened. She stopped making beds and ran downstairs and practically ran into Phillip as he rounded the corner of the hall to go upstairs.

"We have it, we have it," he shouted.

"What are you talking about?" asked Marilee.

"Our application has been approved for our winery, and we can start building as soon as the dig is completed," Phillip added. He was so excited he could hardly talk.

"This is good news," said Marilee. "Do Mike and Dave know?"

Phillip explained he had just left a message to get over here as soon as possible. "I didn't want to tell them in a message. I hope they don't think someone is in trouble," he added.

The back doorbell rang, and Dave and Mike walked in calling Phillip as they walked through the kitchen.

"Is everyone all right here?" asked Dave when he saw both Phillip and Marilee.

"It can only get better," said Phillip. "We got our license. Let's go sit on the patio and talk about this," he continued.

The mood on the patio was happy but serious as the discussion soon turned to planning and organizing the archaeological dig. Dave had already contacted a company to do the dig and just needed to give them a date to fit them into their schedule. Hopefully, it wouldn't be a long wait. A meeting was set up so they could start discussions with the contractor, and as soon as the dig was completed, they could start breaking ground for the foundation. The good news really was that renovations on the old barn could now be started.

Within a week, the contractors arrived and began turning the old barn into the tasting room for the winery. Phillip was happy to get started on something as the group who were to do the archaeological dig were not available until next month. The worker would start removing some of the interior walls that had been constructed when part of the barn had become a winterized workshop.

The main part of the barn was built after the War of 1812, but one small part of it was the original barn the Van Every family had built after they finished their home. It likely dated back to late 1700s or early 1800s. This part was to become Phillip's office and be decorated in the Regency style. At the moment, it had very worn brown panelling on the walls, and there were a number of spots where critters had chewed through to get inside.

The first day was messy and dusty and noisy, but by late afternoon, all was quiet on the demolition scene. Phillip walked to the barn to see if everyone had left but noticed cars still at the site. When he arrived inside, the men were standing around looking at something.

"What have we got here?" asked Phillip.

The crew boss turned and showed him what they were looking at. "We found these behind this wall and thought they might interest somebody. It seems like everyone in this town loves historical artifacts especially this year."

Phillip took the papers and saw it part of the newspaper the *Upper Canada Gazette* dated 1805. As far as the group could make out, it seemed as though it was a want ad for a slave. The paper was quite ragged and faded, but it had been type set and printed. No one knew what to say.

Finally, Phillip said, "I was aware that there were Blacks in the area, but I thought they had all been given their freedom." He took the silence to mean that no else knew anything about it either. "I have to show this to Marilee as she's the history person. If you find anything else, please save it for me. I really don't think this means we can't continue with the restoration, so just keep working and keep your eyes open for something unusual."

Phillip knew as soon as he told Marilee about the discovery she would go into high gear trying to discover who put it there. He decided to wait until after dinner to show her the want ad.

Later that evening after dinner, Phillip showed the paper to Marilee. She didn't get as excited as he thought she might, and then she told him why.

"Jeannie and I discovered information about the Blacks in this area and how there were slaves in some of the homes here in Niagara," she said. "There was an act passed in 1793 by King George III to prevent bringing any more slaves into the area and to set a time line for serving their present masters. Of course, many owners did not agree with the act and continued to buy and sell slaves to their friends and former enemies across the river. It made for an interesting town as freed slaves could be living in close proximity to a current slave owner, and this practice continued for over thirty years."

Marilee then told Phillip about how they were trying to find out whether the farmhand on the Van Every land was a slave or had been freed. She explained how he was the one who delivered Hannah's letters to Peter.

"Have you found out anything more?" asked Phillip.

"Not yet, but we may have some time to check things out next week," replied Marilee. "I might take this paper to the museum with me when we go if that's OK," she added.

"Sure, and we are going to keep a look out for anything else behind the walls," Phillip told her.

The conversation then turned to how long the demolition phase would last and when the actual renovation might start. Phillip explained the new materials were being delivered at the end of the week, so next week there should be something visual happening. It was all very exciting for them both but also tiring, keeping everything organized.

It was after eleven when they climbed the stairs to bed hoping that Hannah would not venture downstairs again tonight. The same guests were still here and seemed fine with the haunting last night, but there was no need to press their luck with another visit.

* * *

Hannah quickly returned to her seat by the window to see if the soldiers were still coming toward the house. She wasn't sure what had just happened or who these strange people were in her house, but at least they were not soldiers. She decided the best way to watch what was going on would be to hide in the dumbwaiter. It had always been a favorite hiding spot where she could read and be away from everyone. Now she just wished she could be with her family.

The dumbwaiter went to the attic, and she was able to slip through the wall and into the shaft and float down to the kitchen. She heard voices and recognized it as her father's. She peeked through the door and saw her parents standing in the kitchen, looking at a soldier who had entered the house. He wore a red coat, brown knee pants, and a black hat on his head. He was carrying a long rifle but had it resting on the floor. Hannah listened to their conversation

"Mr. Van Every, you must come with us tonight and be a part of the British militia as we think the Americans are ready to attack," the soldier stated loudly. "If you do not come tonight, you will be arrested as a traitor and sent to prison. You will only need one set of clothing and your own boots. Do you have a gun?"

"I have my hunting rifle, but my family needs it to hunt food," Mr. Van Every said.

"If you have a son, he will be asked to come as well," the soldier interrupted.

Hannah heard her mother gasp as her father said, "He is not yet twelve."

"He may stay here for now. Go and collect you belongings. You will be issued a gun at the fort," the soldier replied. He then turned to Hannah's mother and spoke in a much softer voice, telling her that she would be wise to take the children and go west into the woods and find a hiding place. There would be a great deal of fighting in this area very soon.

Mrs. Van Every thought about all the wild animals in the woods as well as Indians and couldn't decide whether staying or going would be the more dangerous thing to do. Right now, she was worried about her husband going with the soldiers to fight. They had already killed her daughter and now were taking her husband whom she might never see again. She tried to remain strong as her husband prepared to leave. As he kissed her goodbye, Mr. Van Every whispered in her ear, "Go as we planned to my brother's place and leave very soon. I love you and always will. We will be together again."

Mr. Van Every looked back and tried to smile at his wife as he marched into the night with the soldiers.

Hannah then saw her mother collapse into a chair, sobbing as if her heart was broken. Hannah could only watch and not offer any comfort to her mother. This was as sad as not ever seeing Peter again, and now her father was gone as well. Soon, her mother would take her brother and sister away, and she would be alone in the house. The only thing left to do was to cry, and so she floated back up to the attic and sat by the window and cried for the rest of the night.

One of the good things about being a spirit was not needing sleep. Hannah was happy about this as she needed to watch her mother every minute now to see when she would leave.

Mrs. Van Every was up very early the next morning packing the bare necessities in a basket and a sack to carry with her. She folded up two blankets to use overnight in the woods and an extra set of stockings for herself and her daughter. For her son, she put in a shirt and some socks. She would have liked to take more, but carrying a heavy basket a long distance would be a problem.

For food, she packed dry biscuits and dried meats. Hopefully they would pass a stream and be able to find water. There might even be some early berries in the woods that they could nibble on as they walked. She decided to stay one more day and leave early the next morning as she had not slept well last night. Today, she would pack up a few treasures and hide them somewhere in the farm house in case the soldiers took over their home. She would also bake fresh bread and make a lunch for their first day on the trail.

As Mrs. Van Every went through the house carefully choosing some of her favorite treasures, sadness descended upon her. Every treasure had a memory attached. The pewter candlesticks that had been rolled up in clothes for the journey from America were once again being packed away with care. These had come from England to America and to their present home in Upper Canada and would one day belong to their son. She now wondered what the future of her children would be like. She continued her search in every room of the house, and each room brought some happy and some sad memories. In Hannah's room, she looked for a small trinket to keep but could only find some lace and yarn in a knitting basket that was left in the now empty room.

After a tiring morning of choosing what to save, Mrs. Van Every needed to find a hiding spot for the treasures. The soldiers would certainly check every part of the house for things to take and sell or trade so it could not be inside. She walked out to the barn and continued around the back. This was the spot where waste was often dug into the ground. There really wasn't a lot of waste on this farm, but often, there were bones from a dead animal or some spoiled food that was unsuitable to feed even the pigs.

In the spring, the farmhands would dig up some of the soil to enrich the kitchen garden. Also the fact that it looked as though it had been dug up might look normal to any farmer. Several medium-size holes were dug up at various spots around the area, and Mrs. Van Every deposited the treasures all wrapped in cloth into the holes. She covered up the packages with soil and spread it around so it would not attract attention. Standing back, she looked at her work and decided it would work and so went back to the kitchen to cook one more dinner in her home she was about to abandon. She could only hope and pray that someday they could all return to this house and life could be once again peaceful.

All the while, Hannah had been watching her and silently thinking about what those pieces meant to the family. Hannah was unable to leave the house, so she had only known her mother had gone into the barn carrying things wrapped in cloth. She wished she could leave the house as then she would follow her mother and brother and sister on their journey, but that was not to be.

Mrs. Van Every, upon returning to the house, went to the kitchen and picked up a handful of papers all neatly folded. Hannah wondered what she was going to do with them, so she followed her as she made her way through the kitchen and into the pantry. Once in the pantry, Mrs. Van Every went to the brick wall at the end and began pulling on several of the bricks in the corner. Hannah was surprised to see a brick come out in her mother's hand. Mrs. Van Every then took the letters and pushed them into the hole where the brick had been. They slid in fairly easily, so Hannah thought there must be a space behind the bricks. Mrs. Van Every then returned the brick and made it sure it was even and not noticeable to anyone looking carefully at the bricks.

Hannah had once heard her mother talking about the safe place for letters but did not know this was what she had meant. Hannah told herself she must remember this spot in case she had to hide something.

The next morning was clear and mild for May and would be a good day to travel. Mrs. Van Every had her two children up, dressed, and fed a hearty breakfast by six. She couldn't help herself as she cleaned up the kitchen so anyone, friend or foe, would know she was a meticulous housekeeper.

As they left through the back door, the tears welled up in her eyes to the point she could not see the path clearly. The children were silent as they knew they would only upset their mother even more if they started to cry. Inside, Hannah was flitting around from window to window to keep them in her sight as they made their way to the woods in front of the house. The last glimpse she had were three small figures disappearing behind the barn and into the woods. There was nothing more to do now, so she returned to the attic window and sobbed and sobbed.

*   *   *

The next several weeks at the B&B ran like clockwork. Guests came, enjoyed themselves, and checked out. Several booked for the same time next year. Marilee had time this week to meet Jeannie, and together they went to the museum to look for more information on slavery in the area. They really hoped to find some names that might give them some clues about who stayed on the farm during the war. They spent the morning searching deeds but found nothing. Over lunch, Marilee casually mentioned about blacks being part of the war.

"Maybe we should look at the different regiments that fought in the war," said Jeannie. "It might give names of the men in each regiment."

Marilee added, "I did see where there was one regiment of just Black soldiers. If we could find out the name of it, we might get lucky. Let's try looking for another hour before we leave town."

They returned to the museum after lunch, and as luck would have it, one of the museum volunteers who had written a book about slavery in the area came into the museum to drop off some materials for a lecture. She knew exactly where to look, and soon, Marilee and Jeannie were listening to the whole story of how Blacks lived and worked in the community, paid taxes, voted in elections, and joined the militia during the war.

Marilee and Jeannie sat bolt upright when they heard this last phrase. "Do you know the names of any of these men who fought in the militia?" asked Marilee.

"There is a record taken from a muster roll and pay list of the Colored Corps," explained Helen. "Because these men wanted to defend their homes, they tried to organize a Corps of Men of Color in the Niagara Region but were never able to gather enough men. They probably became part of another larger unit. They did fight at Queenston Heights and Stoney Creek, both British victories, and also worked at Fort George until discharged in 1815."

"Are their names written down anywhere?" asked Jeannie. If you could point us to the right spot, we could look for them and not take up your time," she added.

Helen loved this subject and was always thrilled whenever anyone showed interest and took them to the archives where military lists were kept. Before she left, she gave Jeannie and Marilee her phone number in case they still had more questions. They thanked her, and after she left, it was decided tea one afternoon with Helen would definitely be arranged. She was a wealth of knowledge and loved to share her passion.

Marilee and Jeannie worked their way through a number of records. There were lots of names of black men, but no one named Joseph. Suddenly, the curator entered the room and said she would be closing in ten minutes. Their intention had been to just spend an hour, but instead, it had been three. They carefully put away all the reports and walked to the front lobby.

"Was it a successful afternoon?" asked Mary.

"Yes, and no," replied Marilee. "We had hoped to find the name of a black man living on a farm along the river during the war."

"There are some more records we have stacked in a room in the basement that don't really fit any of our categories of reports," said Mary. "We hoped our summer student might work on them during August, but you are welcome to browse through them whenever you want," she added.

This news fuelled their interest, and once again, they became excited about finding Joseph's whereabouts during the war.

"We'll be back," they both answered.

That night at dinner, Marilee told Phillip what they did and didn't find out. Phillip was very interested in this subject and commented that he might come with them to look up information as well.

Marilee wasn't sure he could help, but she encouraged him to come along tomorrow afternoon.

"Unfortunately, that won't work as the designer is meeting us here at two so we can make some choices of materials for the interior of the barn," said Phillip. "I would really like your help with this."

"Oh, I forgot about that meeting," replied Marilee. "I will be here and arrange another day to look for Joseph."

By now, everyone knew about Joseph. It was as though he was a long-lost relative that everyone wanted to return.

It was late when Marilee and Phillip headed up to bed. It had been silent in the attic since the episode of Hannah coming downstairs, and Marilee hoped this would continue tonight. One of the guests had heard a rumor in town about Loyalist House being haunted and confided to Marilee that she hoped it was not true as she was really frightened of ghosts. She stated she would be requesting a refund if she heard anything as it hadn't been advertised on the website.

Marilee assured her there was nothing to worry about as their spirit liked the attic better than anywhere else. She hoped this would satisfy the guest, and she said her nightly prayer asking for peace and quiet in the attic.

*   *   *

Hannah, however, was keeping a serious lookout for any movement outside or on the river. She was desperate to see someone she recognized. Hopefully it would be Peter or her family.

Tonight, she sat at the window rocking to and fro, hugging her knees. Most of the time, the house was deathly quiet; but every once in a while, there was music playing and people talking and laughing. She was hesitant to go downstairs anymore especially after the scare she had the last time. She did venture down in the dumbwaiter one day when she heard music but only saw a young woman dressed like a man in strange clothing working in the kitchen. Her pants were blue and looked like a second skin, and she was wearing a very tight short top similar to what her brother wore as underwear.

The person was singing a song that had no harmony, and the words made no sense but just kept repeating the same thing over and over. It all seemed very odd to her, so she returned to the attic to keep watch at the window

Suddenly, she saw something move outside. Hannah sat up and saw it was a man walking from the direction of the barn toward the house. It looked like Joseph, the nice farmhand who delivered her letters to Peter. But why was he wearing a militia uniform? Also, why would he be coming to the house when her family was away? The farmhands never came in the house, just to the back door to deliver things.

Hannah decided to float downstairs and see what he was doing. Maybe he would be able to see her, and she could find out about Peter.

Hannah watched as Joseph came into the kitchen and carefully took some dried food from the cupboard. He wrapped it in a cloth and stuck it in his pockets. Hannah was horrified as he was stealing from her family. Joseph then began to search in the desk and other cupboards for something. Hannah must stop him. She began flitting about the room, coming near him and trying to distract him. He lifted his arm to brush something away but continued to search.

Finally, he found what he was looking for—paper, pen, and ink. He sat at the kitchen table and began slowly and carefully to write a letter.

Dear Mr. Van Every,

I have joined the Colored Corps to fight for the British. I found another free man who will look after the farm. I hope to return and find you back here. Thank you for your kindness.

Joseph Jackson

Hannah floated over his shoulder and read as he wrote. He was not stealing but instead sending her father a message. She watched him carefully replace the pen and ink in the desk. He folded the letter and left it on the table. Then he was gone, leaving the kitchen as he had found it.

Hannah watched out the window as he walked to the road and headed toward the fort. Now he was gone too. She picked up the letter and reread it and decided it might not be safe in the kitchen if the soldiers came to the house. She might hide it in the pantry, but right now, she wanted to keep it with her. Instead, she returned to the attic with the letter in her hand and would hide it later.

Once again, she sat at the attic window and rocked back and forth, holding the letter. This was her only connection with the world she used to know.

Tonight, she was too tired and lonely to even cry, but tears streamed from her eyes until the letter in her hand was damp.

AUGUST

Marilee breathed a huge sigh as she returned from the dining room with some empty serving dishes. "Thank goodness Hannah behaved herself last night," she told Julie. "Mrs. Destin said if she heard any 'ghost noises' last night, she wanted a refund for the room as she is afraid of ghosts. Apparently, she heard a rumor about a ghost here at Loyalist House while talking to someone in town. This is what I was worried about if the news became public knowledge, and now it's starting to happen. I wonder where she heard about Hannah."

"I could ask her if you want me to when I take the entree in," Julie offered.

"Well, I would love to know, but we can't be too obvious, or she might get upset again. Only if the subject comes up or nearly comes up," said Marilee.

Breakfast preparations continued, and as Julie took the frittata in to the guests, she looked back at Marilee and whispered, "Wish me luck."

As Julie put the individual asparagus frittatas at each guest place, she listened to the topic of conversation going on around the table. It was one of the favorite subjects—wineries. Several guests were talking about wineries they had visited the previous day and which wines were the best. Mrs. Destin began to describe the winery they had visited, and her detailed description of the architecture and the signature wine let Julie know exactly where she had been.

Then Mr. Destin added, "And that's where we found out this Band B is haunted by a ghost who died here. The owner told us it was a young girl and that she often comes down to the main part of the house screaming."

Julie couldn't help herself and asked Mrs. Destin, "Did you hear any strange noises last night?"

"No, but I was very tired and had wine with my dinner," she said.

"Well, it could just be a rumor," added Julie as she returned to the kitchen. "I didn't even have to ask," she said to Marilee. "Mrs. Destin described Fox Hollow winery perfectly and said the owner told them during their visit. Isn't Fox Hollow the one winery who opposed your application for a winery when you applied to the town?"

"I'm not sure," answered Marilee. "I'll ask Phillip. He'll know who it was."

"I'll ask Dave as well," said Julie. "He might know why they are so opposed to Loyalist House."

That morning at checkout, Marilee asked, as she always did, if everything had been satisfactory and had they enjoyed their stay. There had never been anyone who complained until today.

"Well," said Mrs. Destin emphatically, "I really did not find it relaxing as I was always worried the ghost girl would come into my room. The breakfasts were fine, and the other guests seemed nice, but I do not think we will be booking here again."

"I'm so glad you enjoyed the breakfast, and we do think we have the best guests ever," said Marilee, trying to remain positive. "Have a safe journey home."

Last year, Marilee would have worried all day about how rude Mrs. Destin was, especially calling Hannah "ghost girl," but now she was just happy to see the guests off and relieved to know they would not be coming for a return visit. Now she had to begin the changeover as a group of seven women were coming in tonight for three days of wine tasting and theater.

By two in the afternoon, the rooms were all ready for the next guests, the laundry was drying nicely on the line, and Marilee was sitting on the patio with a glass of iced tea planning menus for the next few days. The crunch of tires on the gravel driveway alerted her to visitors. She thought it was her guests arriving but was surprised to see three cars with several people in each car drive right to the area beside the garage. One of the cars was pulling a trailer. Just as she got up to go and greet them, Phillip came out from his office. He knew the man getting out of the car and quickly introduced him to Marilee.

"Mr. Warren, this is my wife Marilee." Phillip then added, "Mr. Warren is heading up the archaeological dig, and I do believe you are hoping to start tomorrow."

"Yes," he replied. "We just want to drop off our equipment and rope off the area today. We will need an area where there is access to water preferably close to the site."

Phillip suggested he show them around as the actual site was across the road. Then they could get set up. The other five people in the group never said a word but followed after the leader like baby ducks following their mother.

Marilee figured they must be students doing a summer job, judging by their age, and hoped they liked hot, dusty work. This job was scheduled to take about three weeks depending on what they found and the weather. This would be an interesting time, and Marilee had mixed feelings about them finding anything historically significant. On one hand, it would be exciting to find a treasure from the 1812s; but on the other hand, that would just delay the start of building the winery structures. Only time would tell.

Right on the dot of four, two cars drove up the driveway bringing the seven women to Loyalist House for their mini vacation. They arrived at the front door and as there often is with a group of this size; it was hard to make out any conversation as everyone seemed to be talking at once, and no one listening.

Marilee managed to get them all registered and to their rooms. She then invited them to happy hour on the patio in about an hour. She would ask about likes and dislikes for breakfast at that time rather than now.

One of the women, Susan, asked where the door at the end of the hall went.

"That just leads to the attic and the private residence part of the house," answered Marilee.

"Are the rooms in the attic used as B & B rooms?" asked Susan.

Marilee thought this was a strange question but said, " There are no guest rooms in the attic. It is just storage." She turned to go downstairs when another guest asked, "Where does the ghost live?"

Marilee was cautious, especially after Mrs. Destin, and replied, "We don't really know but think she may be in the attic at times. She rarely comes down, and nobody has ever seen her. I will tell you her story at happy hour."

They seemed satisfied for now. Marilee would reveal facts about Hannah later in order to keep rumors under control. She was beginning to feel very protective of Hannah and her story. She didn't want to have anything happen to scare Hannah away or make her angry. She was starting to feel Hannah was part of her family. The dreams of someone sobbing in the night didn't even bother her too much anymore, except for the fact it scared some of the guests. There were just so many questions still unanswered right now.

Phillip had the patio all set up for happy hour, and one by one, the guests appeared. All were settled with some wine, and the local cheeses were being tried. Marilee asked where they were headed the next day, and their whole itinerary for the three days was revealed. They had tickets for three theater shows and wanted to go to at least four or five wineries, plus do some shopping in town. This was quite ambitious planning. Phillip suggested some wineries to visit which would give them a good variety of wines and architectural interests. He deliberately left Fox Hollow off the list.

Susan then asked Marilee to tell them about the ghost.

"How did you know we have a ghost here at Loyalist House?" asked Marilee.

"We have friends who stayed last year, and they told me about the noises at night," Susan replied. "Three of us are part of a group who go to known haunted places and set up cameras to track the ghosts. When we heard about this place, we wanted to come and see what we could find. I hope you will let us set up our equipment in your attic tomorrow night. You can be there with us if you want."

Marilee was so flabbergasted she couldn't speak. She also didn't know how to answer but wanted to scream "no, keep out" as loud as she could. Instead, she calmly stated, "The attic is not licensed as part of the B&B, so guests are not allowed up there." This was the only thing she could think of on the spur of the moment. "Let me tell you the story of Hannah and why we think she is still here."

Marilee then proceeded to tell the group about the War of 1812 and how Hannah had probably died. She gave them more of a history lesson than a ghost story and did neglect to tell them about her dreams. They seemed diverted from their request, and Marilee hoped they had accepted no as an answer.

After a few more questions about the area and points of interest, the group left for dinner in town. Marilee was worried they might try to go to the attic, so she quickly went up and checked that the attic door was locked. It didn't look like a really secure lock, but she thought any lock might discourage them.

There were no disruptions over night from the living or the nonliving, and Marilee felt relieved that the women had accepted her answer. The talk at the breakfast table was all about their bicycle tour to several wineries. Just then the doorbell rang, and when Marilee answered it, the owner of the cycle shop was here to deliver seven bicycles. He would get them out of the truck and asked that the women come out to listen to a safety demonstration as soon as they were finished breakfast. It didn't take long for breakfast to end today, and in less than an hour, the group were ready to go on their tour. This would be an easy day for Marilee and Julie, and things at the B&B should be all spruced up by noon.

Phillip had been up early as he wanted to greet the group doing the dig. He went to the site and saw a very quiet group going about their set up. Ropes were staked out dividing the site into squares, and each person went to their own square and began digging with what looked like a spoon. "This might not be as exciting as I imagined," said Phillip to himself. It looked like they knew what they were doing as no one asked questions or talked to the others in the group. He wondered if anyone found an artifact, they would get excited and call out "Eureka!" After about ten minutes, he decided to go back to his office to work on other matters. The designer was coming later today, and he needed to have all the plans in order.

It was a nice feeling for Julie and Marilee to not have to rush through everything in their clean up. In fact, they worked together today and enjoyed chatting with each other. Marilee told Julie where she was in her search for Peter and Joseph, and Julie told her about a new vine her brother was planting in hopes of harvesting a new type of grape in several years.

After the cleanup, they both went to the kitchen and began part of the preparation for tomorrow's breakfast. It seemed as though the time went quicker, but the work had taken the same amount of time as it always did. They just enjoyed it more.

Today was the meeting with the designer. All the materials, colors, and furnishings for the barn had to be decided so the interior work could get under way. The meeting was planned for two in the barn. The designer, Lisa, arrived on time carrying a large number of sample books. It looked like a lot of decisions would be made today. Introductions were made, and Lisa got right down to business.

"Let's start in the main tasting room as that's the largest room," Lisa said. "What feeling would you like to project there? Modern, traditional?"

Marilee answered, "We talked about this and decided we wanted to keep the historic aspect as the barn is old but include some modern touches, maybe through the lighting and art work."

"I like that idea, and I actually drew up some elevation sketches with some ideas for lights and built-ins using both of those periods," replied Lisa.

They all looked at the sketches, which included lighting plans, flooring, and surface materials. Some choices were accepted and some rejected and other materials selected. The room should give quite a visual impact when customers walked through the front door into the winery. The modern lights hanging from the ceiling would give sparkle and light to the room. The heavy wooden serving fixtures would give weight to the building and ground the room. The trim around the ceiling and all the shelving would emphasize the historic aspect. The requisite historic pictures of 1812 heroes, alongside some modern artwork, would finish off the room.

It took several hours, and the process was repeated for each room in the tasting barn, but finally, all the decisions had been made. It would be fun to watch the interior take shape from flat pictures to dimensional finished rooms.

The women returned from their bicycle tour late in the afternoon and announced they would not be there for happy hour today as they had an early dinner and theater tickets this evening. Marilee thought to herself that after a full day of bike riding, dinner, and the theater, they would be exhausted, so tonight would be a quiet one. She heard the women come in from the theater just before midnight, and they all went upstairs immediately. She too went off to bed, pleased that all was quiet.

Marilee and Phillip awoke with a start.

"What time is it?" asked Phillip.

Marilee grabbed her glasses and looked at the clock. "Good grief," she said. "It's 2:00 a.m."

They both hurried out of bed and into their dressing gowns and proceeded to the guest area where they had heard the screaming.

Five of the seven women were standing by the open door to the attic. They were all wearing running attire and did not look like they had been sleeping. It looked as though they were about to go up the attic stairs.

"What's happening?" demanded Phillip. "How did this door get open?"

Mary Beth turned and sheepishly said, "We were going up to see why Susan screamed."

Marilee immediately pushed through the women and began to climb the stairs. "Everyone, stay down here," she said.

When she reached the top of the stairs, she was horrified to see Susan and Ann standing behind a camera on a tripod. The trunk had been opened. Nothing was taken from it, but it was sitting in the middle of the room. She tried to remember where it was the last time she had been in the attic but couldn't really remember right now. She just knew she was very angry and tried to calm herself before she spoke.

After several deep breaths, she asked, "Why are you two up here?"

Susan began to apologize. "We know you said this was off limits, but we thought we heard scraping noises, so we came up here with our camera. We are so sorry, but just as I was about to leave, I saw something white flit across the room in front of the window."

"Was the trunk open when you came up here, or did you open it?" Marilee asked.

"It was open and in this spot when we got here," replied Susan. "I'm so sorry. When I saw the white film, I screamed, and then everyone downstairs began screaming. We had the camera on but nothing is showing up on it," she continued.

"Well, I think we can just take the camera back downstairs and call it a night," said Marilee as she walked over to the window. She quickly scanned the vista down to the river, but there was nothing out of the ordinary. She continued to watch as the group took the camera downstairs. After they had all gone back downstairs, Marilee quietly said, "Hannah, everything is all right. The intruders are gone, and the attic is yours again."

She hoped this would appease Hannah, and she wouldn't disappear. Marilee left the trunk in the middle of the room with the lid open and went back down the attic stairs.

The group of seven women standing in the hallway looking at the floor reminded Marilee of her teaching days when she had found students guilty of some misdemeanor. If she hadn't been so mad, she might have laughed. She looked around and noticed Phillip had disappeared and wondered why he had left her to deal with this situation.

The women once again all apologized and were heading to their rooms when Phillip reappeared carrying a very large padlock. He locked the door and fastened the padlock to the handle. He put the key in his pocket and said, "I don't think anyone will remove this unless they have super powers."

There was nervous laughter all round, and the women returned to their rooms and shut the doors.

"I just bet they all end up in one room talking about it as soon as we leave," Marilee said quietly as they returned to their quarters. "The conversation should be very interesting at breakfast in the morning, and I bet they don't come for happy hour tomorrow."

Of course, both Phillip and Marilee were so keyed up neither of them could sleep. Sitting in bed, Marilee told Phillip about the trunk being in the middle of the room and lid open and wondered what Hannah was up to. Phillip suggested she might be getting too protective and too involved in the whole story, but he could understand it.

"Are you still having the dreams about her?" he asked.

"Not as often," she replied. "When I do, they are much more vivid and include all the details of the surroundings. She seems to be stuck alone in this house, and all her family and farmworkers have left because of the war. I really don't know whether she will leave too. Are ghosts able to travel to different buildings?"

"I have no idea," said Phillip sleepily. "I am ready to go to sleep, and you should too as morning is coming quickly."

Marilee turned off the light, but her mind was working overtime. She tried the deep breathing exercises, but it wasn't really working. After what seemed like an eternity, she fell asleep, but she could see Hannah pacing in the attic.

* * *

Hannah was agitated. Ever since Joseph had left, it had been very quiet, but tonight was different. She had been sitting by the kitchen window, watching as usual when suddenly she saw movement near the river.

Quickly, her eyes focused on the dock and beyond. Maybe it was Peter. The night was very dark as there was no moon. Even the stars were not shining as brightly as they often did. Suddenly on the river, a boat with a number of men in it passed the dock, then another. The river was being used as a path tonight. She went quickly back to the attic as that was the best place to watch the river. By this time, there was another group of boats passing by the dock.

"That's a lot of soldiers," thought Hannah. "Let's hope they are British." But then she thought that maybe Peter's father might be one of them. She did not want him to be hurt, even though she was annoyed at him for moving across the river. She even wondered if Peter had changed his mind and was now fighting with the Americans.

Hannah realized she was dead, but still in the back of her mind, she thought things would be resolved, and she would eventually return to the pleasant life she used to know. In her present state, she had not accepted the finality of death and could not move forward to another more peaceful place or return to the past. She was stuck in between the living and the dead and could only observe from the vantage point of a spirit.

As she watched the river, her thoughts wandered, and she began to think about her mother and brother and sister. "How many days had it been since they left?" She had never been to visit her uncle William's property, so she couldn't imagine what it might be like. "Would the soldiers go that far and make it an unsafe place for her mother?"

The sound of guns firing quickly brought Hannah's attention back to the river. She looked out again and saw more boats than before, all stopped right in front of their dock. They now looked like they were heading back up the river again. Several guns had been fired, but it was quiet now. They must be gathering to attack somewhere, but Hannah had no idea as she hadn't been able to listen to any adult conversations lately. She decided to just sit by the window and watch. Hopefully, they wouldn't come up on her property or to the house.

*　　*　　*

Breakfast was a quiet affair the next morning. Marilee told Julie about the rendezvous in the attic, and they both wondered what the guests' reaction would be at breakfast. All seven women arrived together for breakfast and quietly sat at the table.

"This so reminds me of a school class who have been caught doing something they weren't supposed to," said Marilee to Julie. "Now they are all on their best behavior."

The both laughed quietly and hoped they could keep a straight face when they went into the dining room.

Marilee took the plate of fruit into the dining room and decided to diffuse the tense situation and came right to the point and asked, "Did you get any movement or sightings on the camera last night?"

Susan was the first to speak. "We have a bit of a white film showing, but I can't tell if it is a ghost or just a shadow. I will look at it more carefully in my dark room when I get home. Also, we are very sorry for disturbing everyone last night, especially since you told us not to go up there. If anything is damaged, let me know, and I will pay for the repairs."

"Thank you for the apology, and no, I don't think anything is broken. The new lock on the door will work for now," said Marilee. "Now what are you all up to today?"

The ice was broken, and several other women began to explain their plans for the day. They were visiting another winery and said for the wine and cheese tonight, they would provide the wine.

"It's the least we can do after causing trouble last night," said Ann.

"That would be lovely," Marilee added. "I will tell Phillip to be ready for you. Now today, we have peach French toast for breakfast as the peaches are at perfection right now. If you are travelling to the wineries, you should stop at a fruit stand and buy some to take home. Most of the farmers, who run the stands, pick the peaches the day before, so you know they are tree ripened and very tasty."

When Marilee returned to the kitchen, Julie whispered, "You are so diplomatic."

"No point in holding a grudge. After all, they may return again next year, and that's five rooms for three nights each. That will pay a few bills," she replied.

Breakfast continued smoothly as if nothing was unusual, and by mid morning, the guests had left for the day. Marilee and Julie were beginning their clean-up routine, and Phillip was out checking on the progress of the dig. Marilee was just putting in a second load of laundry when Phillip came storming into the kitchen and called her several times.

Marilee thought something drastic must have happened to someone and quickly ran downstairs.

"Someone went into the dig area last night and began digging in the site. They have ruined one site completely and have partially damaged the second one," he exclaimed. "I am calling the police as that is trespassing."

Marilee was speechless, which didn't often happen, and could only listen as Phillip related the story. Julie had come running as well as she thought someone must be hurt.

Phillip said several small artifacts had been found yesterday, and they were hoping to find more today. Mostly, they were broken buttons from soldier's coats, but several household items were found as well. There was a spoon and a piece of broken crockery. Most of these items did not constitute a significant find as items like buttons and crockery were found throughout the area on a regular basis.

"How did anyone know about this?" Marilee interrupted.

"That's what we have to find out," he said. "Work has stopped for now which will delay us and cannot continue until the police come. Now I have to call the police so we can get this investigation started."

"This is weird that two things like this would happen at the house on the same night. You don't think they are connected, do you?" Julie asked Marilee.

"I have no idea, but it is strange," she replied. "At least the clean-up process is always consistent and predictable." She laughed as she returned to the laundry room.

Within an hour, the police arrived and knocked on the front door. When Marilee answered, she asked them to drive across the road to the site, and they would find Phillip waiting for them. She really didn't want a police car sitting in the driveway in plain view from the road. She decided to let Phillip handle this issue as she was just about to start some baking for tomorrow. Although she really was curious as to how this trespassing would be handled by the police.

Phillip was glad to see the police arrive and just wanted to get this investigation going so the dig could start again. He told the police everything he knew and answered all their questions with the little bits of information he had. The police decided they needed to interview all the workers on the dig site before they left. By the time they finished, it was late afternoon, and then they continued looking for more evidence around the site. The dig supervisor decided to call it a day and sent the workers home. He did check with the police to ask if they would be able to work tomorrow.

Much to Phillip's annoyance, the police informed him noone was allowed back on the site for two days. After all the workers left, the constable in charge turned and said to Phillip, "We think this may have been initiated by one of the workers, so we are posting a man here overnight to watch for any trespassers tonight."

Phillip was stunned to hear this and said, "This is supposed to be a reputable company, and they have done a number of digs here in town and come highly recommended."

"During a dig two months ago in town, a similar thing happened, and although we were not able to make any connections, we have been watching several people," Constable Jones said quietly. "Where do you keep the artifacts that have been found already?"

Phillip said the supervisor had them, and he assumed he took them home for safekeeping.

"Because they are legally yours, you should have possession of them."

"I was not aware of that point," answered Phillip.

"We can deal with that item tomorrow as I will be calling on Mr. Warren again," Constable Jones said. "I will be in touch with you tomorrow afternoon about four."

"Great, thanks. How will I know who is watching the site tonight?"

"It will be an undercover officer, and he will check in with you when he arrives. He will be in an unmarked car, and he will show you his identification when he contacts you here at the house." Constable Jones turned to leave but then returned and said, "We know you are running a B&B, so we will try and be discreet so as not to scare the guests."

You should have been here last night to scare the guests, and they might not have been so bold," Phillip said, more as a joke.

Suddenly, Constable Jones was interested in what happened last night. Phillip told him about the episode in the attic and had to explain about Hannah's presence. Then Constable took out his notebook and began writing down everything Phillip told him from whom the people were, to what time it happened. He was very noncommittal about the information but said he would check out a few names.

Phillip wasn't really crazy to tell Marilee about this last part, so he decided to just give her the details about the dig. He might try and ask some poignant questions, though, tonight at happy hour.

The rest of the day went slowly, and not much was accomplished by anyone. Marilee wanted to know all about the trespassers and what would happen next. The work on the dig had ended probably until next week, and Phillip was busy thinking up questions to ask their guests that wouldn't make him look too nosey.

He also wondered what kind of wine they would bring as a peace offering. He hoped it was a good one rather than chardonnay or rose. "I really am becoming a wine snob," he said to himself.

The women arrived with the wine right on time. Phillip and Marilee had the nibblies ready, and they all walked to the patio. Since they were not sure what wine was going to appear, Marilee has assembled two platters of food. The pairing for the white was a simple pesto dip with the French bread slices, sliced apples, and a bowl of almonds. The other platter was a bowl of walnuts and some fresh vegetables with a cream cheese rosemary dip.

The wines the group brought were a full-bodied merlot, a pino gricio, and a riesling/chardonnay. "Good choices," thought Phillip.

Everyone was being so polite and cheerful; Phillip had to keep the questions light, or he might be in trouble with Marilee.

"How many times have you visited this area?" he asked.

Susan answered that she had been here four times as had two others in the group, but this was the first time for Ann and Peggy.

"Where did you stay the other times?"

"We stayed in a hotel a couple of times, but last year, we stayed at the B&B right next to Fox Hollow winery."

Phillip almost choked on his wine but recovered in time to ask, "Why did you not stay there this year?"

The women went on to say they didn't really like all the rules at Fox Hollow, and a continental breakfast was all that was served. "Your breakfasts are so much better," said Peggy.

Marilee was listening to this conversation and wondered why Phillip was so interested in where people stayed and why. This was so not like him. She also wondered what rules Fox Hollow had and if the group had broken any and was maybe not welcome back. She thought it wise not to ask, though, as everyone seemed in a good mood, and she didn't really want to bring up last night's episode.

Dinner plans had been made, so the group thanked Phillip and Marilee for the hospitality and left. As soon as they were well out of hearing range, Marilee asked Phillip why he had asked such strange questions. Phillip then told Marilee about Constable Jones comment about a previous dig, and there would be an undercover officer on duty overnight on the property.

Marilee was horrified. Now she not only had to worry about whether people knew there was a ghost on the property but also that trespassers were coming on to their land and stealing. She knew she would worry all night about this. She couldn't say much more to Phillip as he would say just let it go. But that wasn't her way of dealing with things. She was quiet all during dinner and retreated to their private quarters to read after all the preparations for morning had been done. She went to bed early, but her mind was racing, and she thought she was still awake but suddenly found herself in the attic watching.

*   *   *

Hannah was sitting on a chair by the window, looking out at the river. Her fingers were picking at threads in the hem of her dress. She would unfold the hem and then turned it back in again and press it smooth with her fingers. She repeated this procedure over and over again along the front of her dress. Her dress was becoming quite tattered along the hem, and even though Hannah told herself she would put holes in the fabric if she kept rubbing it, she could not help herself.

She could see boats going up the river, but there was no gunfire, just soldiers riding in the boats. Periodically, there was a barge carrying equipment as well as the troops. She still was unable to identify whether the soldiers were friend or foe. The darkness and the quietness made Hannah begin to miss her mother again. She began to wonder if they had made it safely to her Uncle's home, and if the soldiers would find them there. As she thought about her family while watching the river a strange feeling seemed to enter her body. If she looked straight ahead at the wall, she could see her mother and brother and sister walking through trees.

Sarah Van Every was encouraging her children to keep walking and keep up the pace. It was almost dark, and they must reach a safe place to stay the night. The last two nights had been spent in the woods hiding under fallen tree branches.

Hannah's brother, Andrew, had cut spruce branches and built a lean-to for protection. The ground was also covered with soft pine needles but was still quite hard for sleeping. The threesome had walked for two straight days stopping at dark and beginning again at first light.

Hannah's sister, Mary, often had to be carried at the end of the day as she was exhausted. Andrew would put her on his shoulders, and within minutes, she would be asleep with her head resting on his. He and his mother took turns carrying her, and Mary did not even wake while they transferred her from one to the other.

Sarah tried to sleep at night but was worried they might be found by either animals, Indians, or the enemy. She let Andrew sleep as she needed him to be alert during the day. She thought about how their life had changed so drastically from enjoying a peaceful and prosperous life on a farm to becoming fugitives running away through the woods.

According to her figuring, she thought they would be to William's farm by dark tonight. Hopefully there would be room for them to stay and no soldiers to cause them to have to leave again. The frightened family had eaten the last of the biscuits and dried meat at midday, and she knew her son, a growing teen, must be starving. She had noticed several times he grabbed at some berries as he passed by bushes in the woods. This would not fill his constantly empty belly for long.

The sun had been their compass over the past three days. She had heard her husband say many times if one left from the turn in the river just north of their property and kept going west with the sun, you would arrive at William's farm. She certainly hoped this was true.

Andrew had walked there once with his father, and he thought they were on the same trail. The sun was just about to go down behind the horizon when a definite clearing appeared ahead. Sarah was carrying Mary, but Andrew saw the clearing and began running to the edge of the woods. He cautiously stopped to see if anyone was in sight. Seeing no one, he waited for his mother, helped transfer Mary to his shoulders, and together they walked into a meadow. They could now see a small building ahead and several other outbuildings set away to one side. As they approached the building that was probably home to this family, the door opened, and they could see a man standing there with a gun in his hand ready to shoot.

Sarah Van Every grabbed Andrew's shoulder and pulled him back behind her. She was close enough now that she recognized William.

"William, it is us. Your brother's family," she cried.

William put down the gun and ran to meet her. He lifted Mary from Andrew's shoulders and carried her to the house, with Andrew and his mother following. Inside, they met a frightened family all huddled together behind a table fearing the worst. When they realized it was William's brother's family, the tension cleared. Sarah knew William but had only met his wife once before. They now had four small children. William's wife, Elizabeth, welcomed them in, made them sit down, and began heating water for tea. She gathered together some meager leftovers from their dinner and put them in a pan to heat up.

Sarah was tired but so relieved to be with family again she could only weep. After some food and warm tea, she relayed the story of her husband being conscripted into the army, his telling her to leave and come here, and of course of Hannah's death. Once again, she began to sob.

Elizabeth put her arms around her and said, "There will be time for talking tomorrow. Now we must get you to bed where you can have a good night's sleep without worrying. The children must be exhausted as well."

Andrew and young Mary were put to bed on the floor next to their cousins and within minutes were asleep. Sarah was given a straw mattress on the floor beside the children, and even though she was used to a feather bed, this felt like heaven to her. She was bone weary after three days of walking, but she thanked God that they had made the journey safely and asked God to keep her husband safe. She was relieved that tonight, some of the fear and worry was gone and she could sleep.

*   *   *

After a night of tossing and turning, both Marilee and Phillip got up early to get the breakfast started. Phillip was waiting all night for the police to knock on his door, but that did not happen. Marilee had watched both Hannah and her mother deal with their issues in her dream. They hoped today would be less stressful. At nine, there was a knock on the kitchen door, and the undercover detective was standing there. He was invited in and given a cup of coffee. He and Phillip went into his office and shut the door. Marilee desperately wanted to be in there but had to continue being the hostess as the guests were still eating breakfast.

Detective Barrens began telling Phillip that someone had come back last night around two and wandered around but had quickly left when he saw a car parked back by the barn. "I managed to get a plate number from the car, and we have a name and address for the owner of the car. Of course, the car could be stolen, but someone at the station is checking it out. I was also close enough to get a rough description of his height and clothing. We will be back again tonight to see if anyone returns."

Phillip thanked him and asked to be kept informed of anything new, knowing very well they could only give him information after everything was checked out. This was becoming more complicated than he thought it would be. "Why would anyone want to steal a few artifacts that could be found just about anywhere?" he asked the detective.

"We have no idea, but people do crazy things," he answered. Detective Barrens left through the kitchen and was pleasantly surprised when Marilee handed him some breakfast in a takeout container. "I like this assignment," he said as he left.

There were no more surprises at breakfast, and the guests left on friendly terms, saying they would return next year. Marilee wasn't sure she wanted them back as guests and just put stars beside their names, identifying them as possible unwanted guests. She would decide next year whether to accept their reservation if they called and asked to stay at Loyalist House.

The rest of the month was busy with guests filling the rooms almost every night. This was the high season, and September was usually the busiest month of the year. There was no time to think about what Hannah was doing in the attic. Whatever it was she seemed to be doing, she was doing it quietly lately, and Marilee found sleeping at night was easy. Maybe it was because she was so tired.

Phillip, though, was not sleeping as he was worried about who wanted to steal from their property and how they were going to overcome the delays because of it. The police were not staying overnight anymore, but he had not heard any news from them. Many nights he was in his office looking through papers, hoping to find some clue, but he didn't. It just made the next day hard to get through, and he hated to admit that an afternoon nap was beginning to look good most days.

Next month was the start of the harvest, and the major part of the interior renovations in the barn would be complete by the end of the month. "It will only get better," he told himself.

SEPTEMBER

This was the month that Marilee loved. Things were busy at the B&B, but the weather was pleasantly warm with just a hint of coolness to it. Many people loved to travel during September as the crowds were a bit smaller, and restaurant reservations were easier to make. Marilee looked at their bookings and noticed there were only about four days during the whole month where they had no reservations. It would be busy. She suddenly remembered that Manfred was supposed to call this month and come to exorcise Hannah from the attic. Marilee needed to talk to Jeannie and decide whether or not they wanted to go through with it.

If she got rid of Hannah, guests would not ask for their money back, and guests who wanted to capture her image on camera might not book at all. And if Hannah stayed, the guests who booked might not be the kind of guests you wanted. It was very complicated.

With that in mind, she called Jeannie, and they scheduled to meet for lunch tomorrow at Have Another Cookie. Now she needed to start planning some menus and baking for the month. At one point, this month, a couple from Bermuda were staying at Loyalist House for six days. That meant six different breakfasts must be planned.

Phillip came through the back door at that point and was smiling. "It looks like we won against the big guys," he said. "The bottling place has agreed to bottle our wine this year and has given us a three-week window in late September to get our grapes to them. With the weather the way it is, we should be able to get the grapes off by that time. Now we just have to arrange for the pickers to get to the vineyards."

Marilee was glad to see Phillip had some good news for a change. He thought no one knew he wasn't sleeping, but Marilee was aware of his nightly visits to his office. She was hoping the intruder mystery would be solved soon.

The group doing the dig had come back and finished their work. It was interesting to note that the group was minus one of the original workers. No one said anything, and no one asked. Now Phillip just had to wait for their report. The diggers had found three arrowheads and the buttons and crockery pieces, so nothing of real significance. Phillip's partner, Dave, said that was a usual find for the area, and they would not be stopped because of such commonly found artifacts. Buttons and arrowheads were apparently found everywhere when people started digging. In fact, the museum did not accept any more of these items as they had plenty. Mostly young boys used them as part of the many games they played.

"When do you think the archaeological report will arrive?" asked Marilee. "Will it have the permission to start construction, or will you have to apply for that as well?"

"The report will just state nothing significant was found, so then we just have to send the report to the town office. The application is completed, except for that report. It is pretty much a done deal but just have to wait for them to get this report and sign off on it," said Phillip. "Hopefully, we will have the OK by the end of the week. Now I'm off to line up the equipment to come and pick grapes. Dave tested the bricks this morning, and they are just about ready."

Phillip was just leaving for his office as the phone rang. Marilee answered it and gave Phillip the signal that it was for her.

The voice on the other end said, "Hello, Marilee. This is Manfred, and I was calling to arrange a meeting time to help you with your spirits in the house."

Marilee was speechless for a moment, even though she knew he would be calling this month. Upon recovering, she said, "Thank you for calling. At this point, we are still unsure what we should do about our resident spirit. She doesn't seem to be causing a lot of trouble, and we did find out who she was. We may decide to let her stay."

"Oh, I am always thrilled to hear people say that, as I think any house with a spirit has so much more charm. But I would really like to come and analyze the situation, and I might be able to find out more about her and who else may be in the house."

Marilee was not ready for that bit of information. "Oh, I think we only have one ghost with us. We haven't heard from any others."

"Often, one is the dominant spirit, and the others stay in the background until it is their turn to take the lead. If there is a great turmoil in the area or the spirits are competing with each other for dominance, that is when you might hear from all of them at one time."

Marilee's mind was going in all directions, and she couldn't think what day would be good to have Manfred out to the house. "When will you be in the area?"

"I have the third week of September open in my schedule and would like to take two days to meet these spirits," he said.

Marilee stalled for time so she could think. "I will have to look at my guest bookings to what days would work. Can I call you back tomorrow and let you know?"

"That will be fine," answered Manfred.

Manfred left his contact information, and when Marilee hung up, she immediately called Jeannie to tell her about the call. They decided lunch would be today instead as they had to decide what to do by tomorrow. Manfred had seemed intent on coming either way, so they really needed to have a plan of their own. Marilee now had to get a whole day's work at the B&B done in the next two hours. She prioritized her list, crossed off a few things that could wait, and started to work.

The doorbell rang at eleven thirty, and in walked Jeannie ready to go for lunch. Luckily, Phillip was going to be around all afternoon, so he would be there if the arriving guests were early. Marilee quickly changed, and off they went already talking about the pros and cons of removing Hannah.

Lunch took two hours, and at the end, both Jeannie and Marilee had decided Hannah had to stay in the house. They would make a decision later about whether to remove any other ghosts unknown to them at this time. Marilee did want to know if there were others, so they would call Manfred and have him come to investigate. Jeannie made Marilee promise that she could be there as this was just too exciting to miss.

The next day, Marilee called Manfred, and a date was set for the third Tuesday of September. There were no guests that day, and Marilee went on the computer and blocked the Tuesday and the Wednesday off so no one could book on line. She needed a few days off anyway as bookings were steady for the whole month. Now she would just have to be patient until the twentieth.

That night after all the guests had checked in and Phillip and Marilee were eating dinner, Marilee told Phillip about Manfred's comment that other ghosts may be in the house.

"Then they better start paying the taxes," joked Phillip. "I don't really care how many live here as long as they don't cause trouble and damage the place."

"So you wouldn't mind if we kept Hannah here? We can wait and see about the others after we find out who they are," replied Marilee.

"Sounds good to me."

The rest of the evening was spent preparing for breakfast, and even though it had been a busy day, Marilee had trouble falling asleep that night. She tried reading for a while and even got up and walked around the house in the dark. Finally, she made some tea and read a bit more and thought she was still reading, but the story suddenly changed.

*   *   *

Hannah had been watching her uncle's house where her mother and brother and sister were staying. She was feeling a bit less agitated as she knew they were safe there. But tonight, something was bothering her. As she looked out the window at the river, she could see the boats carrying both British and American soldiers up and down the river. Sometimes, there were natives passing quietly along in canoes as well.

"Something must be going to happen soon. I must get to the front of the house to see if any men are on the road."

She once again traveled carefully down the dumbwaiter to the kitchen and crept to the dining room where she could see out the front windows. She was horrified to see a group of men, maybe twenty, heading up the lane toward the house. She carefully hid herself in the pantry between the kitchen and dining room and hoped no one would find her. She still forgot sometimes that she was invisible to living people. The men were now on the porch and trying the front door. It was locked, but suddenly, a click sounded, and the door opened. They were not dressed in uniforms but were wearing regular clothing that was now ragged and dirty. These did not look like soldiers, except they were carrying guns.

One of the men removed his hat and spoke, "Please don't take things, just come to the kitchen, and we will hopefully find some food."

Hannah gasped. It was her father. Why was he with these men?" She stepped out of the cupboard and followed them to the kitchen, remembering now that they couldn't see her. These must be part of the militia that her father joined, but why didn't he have a uniform? Why was he home? Was the war over?" She decided to listen to their conversations to find out what was happening.

David Van Every found some dried food in the cupboard and put it out on the table. The men quickly devoured anything edible. They did not start a fire in the stove as they did not want their presence discovered by anyone on the river.

Their conversations indicated they were on their way to help the British fight off any Americans crossing the river from Fort Niagara. The march would take several days, and there was no food supplied to them by the British. It was expected they would raid houses on the way.

It was late afternoon, and Hannah heard her father suggest they stay in the house overnight, gather any vegetables left in the garden, and leave before dawn. They would take turns keeping watch on the river for Americans. The men seemed to listen to him and follow his orders, but she was still worried they might go through the house and steal anything they felt was valuable. She watched her father as he walked from room to room looking at each room and quietly remembering things and events that had taken place here during peaceful times.

At one point, he was holding a dish from the sideboard, and Hannah thought she saw him wipe his eyes. "Was he crying?" She went close to him, but he did not notice anything or look in her direction. What she really wanted to do was hug him, but she knew that wouldn't work. This made her very sad, and she felt like going to the attic and crying, but she couldn't make herself leave the room where her father was. She would watch over him all night and guard the house in case any of the other men decided to take anything.

All night, Hannah hovered over her father as he slept and followed him as he walked around the house. The men took turns sleeping and keeping watch and seemed to be very mindful that this was not their house or their property. She guessed most of these men were farmers in the area and had been conscripted by the British to join the militia just as her father had. It could be any of their houses they were entering to find food and shelter.

Very early before it was light, the men all arose, grabbed any bits of dried food they could carry, and prepared to leave. David Van Every was the last to leave, and when everyone was outside, he went to the pantry and took the brick from the wall. He reached in and took some of the papers that Hannah had seen her mother put there before she left. Mr. Van Every read them and replaced them. He then took some other papers from the very back of the hiding spot and replaced the brick. He did not take time to read these papers but put them in his pocket as he walked to the front door. He took one last look and closed the door.

Hannah heard the lock click and knew he was gone. She began to sob as she watched the men walk down the lane to the river road. Twice she saw her father turn around and look back, and she wondered if he could hear her sobbing.

* * *

Marilee awoke with a start. She was still sitting in the wing back chair in their family room. Her book was on her lap at page 178, and her cup of tea, now cold, sat partially full on the table beside her. It was 5:00 a.m. She had slept there all night dreaming about Hannah. She remembered hearing the sobbing but only before she woke up. What was going on now to make Hannah suddenly begin sobbing again?

"Well, here we go again," she thought. "I might as well get up and start the day."

Marilee definitely needed a hot shower to wake her up this morning. Coffee would help as well. Within a half hour, she was downstairs starting the breakfast preparations and drinking coffee when Julie arrived to help.

"You're up early today," said Julie. "Don't tell me there were problems in the attic again."

Marilee described her dream to Julie and told her about sleeping in the chair.

"As well I have to call Manfred, the ghost buster, to let him know we have decided to keep Hannah."

Julie had not been at the B&B for three days, so Marilee filled her in on all the details about extra ghosts and what they might do with them if they were discovered.

"You have to let me be here when this guy comes to perform the exorcism. I can't even imagine what he would do."

"If anyone else finds out about this, we may have the whole town here to watch. Yes, you can come, but don't tell anyone else."

"I promise," said Julie while giving the girl guide salute.

Breakfast proceeded, and the six guests staying at Loyalist House were delightful. Once again, they were all friends traveling together and had come to town to enjoy several plays. They were thrilled when Phillip invited them to happy hour on the back patio this evening.

Marilee whispered to Julie when they were alone in the kitchen that Phillip was always the hero as he waltzed in halfway through breakfast, told them humorous stories, and then invited them to join him for drinks on the patio. "How could anyone not like him?"

"Well, you know we're not too fond of him in her cooking, so we'll let him play the part of the charmer."

Life at the B&B continued as usual. There were no more nights of sobbing that Marilee heard. No guests complained of strange noises, the guests from Bermuda were thrilled with a different breakfast all six days, the laundry was washed and ironed, and the house was spotless as always. Marilee kept herself busy trying not to think ahead to the day Manfred was coming.

During this time, Phillip kept close watch on the mail; and finally one day, the letter he was waiting for arrived. The archaeological dig had been inconclusive with no significant artifacts found on the site. He was thrilled that they would now be able to begin building the winery work buildings but somewhat annoyed at the several thousand dollars spent finding out nothing. Now the real work would begin, and by next spring, Loyalist House B&B and Winery would be a reality. His next step was to call Dave and Mike and invite them over to celebrate and begin planning for real.

As he hung up the phone, the doorbell rang. "I don't think any guests are coming in today," he said, mostly to himself.

When he opened it, Detective Barrens was standing there with a large envelope in his hand. "Good day, sir. I have some interesting news for you about the break in at the dig site."

"Come in, let's sit in the kitchen where it's quiet and private. I'll call Marilee as I'm sure she would like to hear the news as well."

Phillip called Marilee and after greetings were exchanged, Detective Barrens said, "We found the person who came into the dig site and disturbed it as well as took some of the artifacts that had been found. It was one of the summer students and some of his buddies who lived around here. They thought they could make a quick dollar by selling some of it. Unfortunately, they forgot to research the value of arrowheads. Since they are always being found, they are virtually worthless. The value of the theft is under two hundred dollars, so it would have to go to small claims court to receive any compensation. However, they could be charged for trespassing on private property if you wish to press charges."

All Phillip could say was "whew."

Detective Barrens then told Phillip and Marilee that the student who had associated with his friends had lost his job and had been expelled from the program at the university. "The job was part of a coop program, but he was being paid. His friends are a different story. They are without work and not in school, and we suspect they are into the drug scene. You can press charges, but we would like to ask you not to so we can watch them and hopefully catch them when they make a bigger mistake that will stick to them. We need to get them off the street."

Phillip and Marilee were speechless but concerned that this kind of behavior was taking place so close to their house. They agreed with the officer and decided not to press charges. Detective Barrens said if any future actions resulted in convictions, he would let them know. He thanked them for their cooperation and left.

"I feel like we are wrapping up a lot of loose ends this month," said Phillip. "The stars must be all aligned in our favor."

"Just one more to go," replied Marilee.

Finally, Tuesday arrived when Manfred was coming to check out how many ghosts were in the house. Marilee was very excited and had not slept at all last night and not because of Hannah's sobbing. She and Julie and Jeannie were drinking coffee about ten thirty when the doorbell rang. Marilee was glad he handed her his card during the introductions as she might otherwise have called for help.

Manfred was about six feet tall, a sturdy build and sported a very full beard and curly hair to his shoulders. He was wearing rumpled chinos with spots here and there and a plaid shirt that was obviously not new. He spoke, though, with a gentle, almost lyrical voice and was very precise with his language. When they were seated in the living room, he began to tell them how he would discover who was living in the house. He always referred to the ghosts as spirits and in a very respectful way.

"First, I would like you to take me on a tour of the house and point out all the places where there have been sightings or an incidence. Then I will go back to those places by myself to discover who is here. I may also feel someone's presence in other place so will return there as well. I would like you all to remain outside while I am seeking the spirits as they often resent my bringing visitors along."

There was nothing Marilee could say but "OK." She then gave Manfred a tour of the house, including the attic and the basement. She also showed him where they had found the letters in the dumbwaiter.

"Do you need to see the doll and the clothes we found in the trunk?" she asked.

"That might be very helpful. You mentioned you found letters. Do you have them here?"

"The originals are downstairs as I have not put them back in the doll yet."

"Yes, I think that would be helpful. Thank you," Manfred answered.

Marilee found all the things Manfred needed, and she and Julie and Jeannie left him alone to do his work. She decided more coffee was not the answer, so even though it was only noon, Marilee took a bottle of 2010 pinot gricio and some cheese and crackers out to the patio to wait.

It was about an hour before Manfred found them on the patio. Marilee offered him a glass of wine, but he declined and just asked for water. He actually looked very tired as if he had done physical work all day. Phillip arrived at that point and joined the group for the results if you could call it that.

Manfred began, "I have found a young girl residing in the attic. She is in love and cannot leave as she is waiting for her fiancé to return. I know she is sad, but her work here is not finished. I'm not sure what it is, but she has to do something before she can move on. I would recommend you let her remain here at the house. She is quite timid and should not cause any trouble other than noise and scaring nonbelievers."

"Wow," said Marilee. "That's exactly what Hannah is like."

Manfred's head snapped around and looking directly at Marilee asked, "How do you know her name?"

Marilee then told him the story of researching the family and how they were pretty sure that's who she was.

He seemed to settle down a bit after the information was given and continued, "There are, however, four other spirits living in various parts of the house, all in the oldest part."

Marilee couldn't seem to breathe but realized she had been holding her breath. Once she took a breath, she was fine and asked, "Who are these people, and when did they come here?"

Manfred continued to tell them. "The spirit in the basement appears to be a manservant based on the clothing he is wearing. He is very old and probably died of old age in the house at one time. I am not sure why he is still here. He mostly sleeps, but it would be nice if he could move on. He may have died during a war and was left behind because of circumstances.

"The second spirit is a middle-aged man of means. He is well dressed and was well fed. He may have been a guest who died while visiting. He seems to be waiting for someone as he is constantly looking at his pocket watch. Based on the clothes, I would say he died about 1890.

"The last two are children about four or five. Their clothes are from a time period about 1910 or later. They probably died of a disease and because of their parent's grief were not able to leave. It would be best to let them go as well."

Marilee could not speak as she had tears in her eyes and was looking for a tissue. When she recovered, somewhat and without even consulting the others, she said, "You must set the four spirits free, but Hannah can stay for now. Possibly in another two years or so, she will have figured out what to do. By 2015, the commemoration of two hundred years of peace with the United States will have ended, and that may be the turning point for her.

"I am unable to continue today as I am tired, but let us arrange another day within the week when I can return and set the spirits free," Manfred said.

Marilee took Manfred to the office where they checked her date book to find a suitable day when there were no guests. It looked like it would have to wait until ten days from now as that was the first break with no guests. Manfred agreed, and the time and date was set and written in the book.

"Why have we never heard from the other spirits?" asked Marilee.

"We don't always know why, but often as the spirits give up hope of ever moving on, they do become weaker. None of them are bad or grumpy spirits, so you are lucky."

Marilee thanked him and said they would see him next week. She returned to the patio where Julie and Phillip had set out leftovers from breakfast and of course, wine for lunch.

Everyone was trying to talk at once, and all were asking questions, but no one was answering. Phillip raised his voice and said, "How did those other ghosts get here, and we never knew about it?"

Marilee added, "Will we hear them now? I don't think I could bear to see small children as ghosts."

Jeannie, for once, was absolutely quiet, but you could see her mind churning all this information around and wondering what to do with it.

Julie just kept saying, "Wow."

Lunch continued with ghosts being the main topic of conversation. The big question now was what Manfred would do to set the ghosts free. Marilee decided she would ask about his methods and of course could they be present. She was pretty sure his answer would be no.

That night, as they were getting ready for bed, Marilee was very nervous. She kept delaying actually getting into bed and turning off the lights.

Finally, Phillip asked, "Are you coming to bed, or are you staying up all night? You know you'll have a better chance of dreaming about this if you are asleep."

"I'm just so worried about seeing the other ghosts, and they may be angry since we disturbed them. What if Hannah is mad that others are here and she leaves?"

"There's not much we can do about that now unless you plan on staying awake for a week."

"I know," said Marilee. "I just don't like sad dreams."

Marilee managed to calm herself enough to get to sleep and in the morning realized she hadn't dreamt at all. The next night, however, was very different.

*　　*　　*

Peter had planned his trip back to the farm in great detail. He knew many people were living outside Fort Niagara, and many crossed the river on a regular basis. It was a chaotic scene and would not be hard to help someone carry loads of supplies across the river. He soon found a kind gentleman who was not strong enough to carry all his supplies by himself.

Peter was careful not to tell anyone his real name and to mumble a bit to disguise any accent he might have. He wasn't sure who sided with whom and didn't want to get involved in the politics of the war. War had been declared a few months ago, but the rumor was that the battles were taking place at the other end of the lake. Everyone knew though that it was only a matter of time before fighting would be here on the Niagara frontier.

Peter arranged to meet his new friend this morning and help him load some cargo onto a barge. If all went well, he would be back at his parents' farm by the week's end.

Everything went as planned, and the gentlemen even gave him a ride in his wagon as far as the edge of the small town. He said he had no money to pay for his help but instead gave him a sack of food to eat on the way to his destination.

The river road at this time was a dangerous path to take as not only were there soldiers marching both ways, but also if the British spotted him, he would be conscripted on the spot for the militia. Peter had full intentions of joining the militia, but first, he needed to get to the farm. The safest way was through the bush along the edge of the river. There were many places to hide, and you could easily see if an unfriendly group were on the river. His only concern was meeting some Indians that were in the woods. He had heard gruesome stories and hoped they were not true. He would just have to take his chances.

Hannah sat up with a start and looked out the window. There was no one on the river, but she sensed something or someone. She quickly floated down the stairs to look out toward the river road. She saw large groups of soldiers walking slowly along the road. They had red coats on, so she knew they were British. She hoped they wouldn't come in the house. They obviously were in no hurry as part of the group would sit down for a while and then get up and move on.

War was a curious endeavor as it seemed very disorganized. If she was in charge, it would be far more orderly, and they would all do everything at the same time. Once they were all out of sight, she returned to the attic to watch and wait.

Peter's journey took the better part of four days. He had now run out of food and was relying on some late berries in the bushes. It was midday, and he began to sense familiar parts of the landscape. In particular, he recognized the turn in the river where the land jutted out and created a point in the river. If he was right, this was at the north end of the Van Every farm. He was sure the Van Everys would be there and understand why he had come back. He hoped they would welcome him into their home until he could get organized again on his farm. He did not realize that most families had fled for safer spots because of the war.

Peter was at the clearing at the edge of the farm when he noticed soldiers walking toward the house. They were wearing red coats, so they must be British. He would have to wait until they left or try to move further south without being spotted. He crept as close as he dared to the house and watched as the soldiers kicked in the front door and entered the house. He was worried about the family and listened carefully but did not hear any screaming or crying or gunfire. They must be gone.

Hannah had heard the front door banging and quickly went back downstairs. She was hiding in the dumbwaiter when she suddenly sensed someone. Were her parents back? No. These were British soldiers ransacking their home, so it couldn't be her father.

Suddenly she had a strange sensation, and a buzzing noise filled her head. She sensed Peter was here. Surely he had not returned and joined the British soldiers. Why was he here? Had he come back to see her? Was he a ghost as well?

Hannah left her hiding spot in the dumbwaiter and began swirling around the kitchen, creating a breeze as she did. She bumped into several soldiers on her way and ran forcibly into others. How dare they steal from her parents' home? She wanted them to leave so she could find Peter. She knew he was somewhere close.

She began to remember she could make terrible screaming noise while flying about. Several soldiers were aware of a presence and became quite frightened by it. Hannah sent a jar crashing to the floor on the other side of the room, and suddenly she had the soldiers' attention. She broke another large platter in front of them and then another. Upon seeing dishes flying off the shelf and breaking and hearing a loud wailing noise, the soldiers decided to retreat and leave the house. Most of them were running at full speed by the time they had cleared the porch heading to the road. A haunted house was not worth raiding.

Hannah, however, was not satisfied just with their leaving. She wanted to find Peter and somehow must get his attention so he would know she was there. She flew around the entire inside of the house wailing as she went. Dishes were flying off shelves and smashing, and furniture was turned upside down. She continued for quite some time but finally gave up as Peter did not appear. She knew he was there. Why did he not see her?

Peter stayed in the bushes until darkness began to settle. From here, he could find his way home in the dark. He now realized everything had changed since he left. His friends were not here; there was no one left on the farm, and possibly their home would be the same. This was not the return he had imagined.

He waited until it was all quiet both on the river and the road to begin his journey to the family farm. It was quite dark now, but Peter knew all the paths by heart. He stopped at the Van Every barn, but there were only a few scrawny chickens roosting on the walls between the stalls. He did check for eggs in a few corners that looked like nests and considered himself lucky as he found one, still warm. He must have beaten the nighttime predators. He walked past the farmworkers' houses, but they were all empty. He might be the only person around that was not military.

Within half an hour, he approached the Gillham farm. The house looked deserted, and since the door was open, Peter figured soldiers had been there looking for anything they could carry away. He thought he spotted some movement in the bushes by the barn. Should he call out his name or try to get around behind the suspect? A quick decision was needed.

"It's Peter Gillham. I have returned home."

"Peter," the voice said as a large man approached him.

Not being sure of being tricked, he had his knife at the ready; but as the figure came close, Peter recognized the farmhand Eli who worked with his father. He was soon swept up into large arms almost lifting him off the ground.

"Where is the rest of the family?" asked Eli. "Why have you come alone? These are dangerous times."

Peter then told him about returning and how he hated being across the river. "My parents do not know where I am. I just left a note saying I was returning to the British side. It is better for them if they do not know. What has happened to the Van Everys and all the workers?"

Eli then told him how the whole family, including workers, had left several weeks ago. "All their animals are here, what's left of them, and we are taking care of them plus those you left behind. Sarah and I and the children are the only ones here. It is very dangerous especially at night, so Sarah and the children have found a hiding place when the soldiers come. Of course, you must come and stay with us in our cabin as your house has been stripped of almost everything."

"Thank you, Eli. I am thankful for your kindness."

As they entered the humble two-room cabin, Eli called to his wife that it was safe to come out. Sarah was in tears when she saw Peter and gathered the bits of leftover food to feed him. She laughed as he pulled the egg from his pocket. The rest of the evening was spent telling each other about their families and what was happening with this war. Even though Peter felt safe in the cabin, his sleep was troubled as he did not know where the future would take him.

*   *   *

Marilee came down to the kitchen in the morning, hoping once again the guests had not been interrupted by the wailing last night. She suddenly stopped when she saw two chairs upside down beside the table and broken dishes on the floor. Her first thought was someone had broken into the house. But after checking the door and seeing the alarm still set, she started to get chills. Was this Hannah's work?

Julie knocked softly on the door and entered and saw the mess. "What happened here?"

"I'm not sure," said Marilee, "but I suspect it might have been Hannah. I had a strange dream last night, and Peter was in it. It must have agitated her, and this is the result. She's never done this before."

"Did you hear any noise down here in the night?"

"I heard noises, but it was mostly someone crying, and I thought it was coming from the attic."

"Do you suppose she is mad about Manfred being here, and maybe it was one of the other ghosts?"

"I don't know, but let me take a picture with my phone, and then we can clean up and start breakfast."

Amazingly, not one guest asked about strange noises at breakfast. Everyone was excited about their plans for the day and thrilled with the delicious French toast and apple/cinnamon topping Marilee was serving.

Marilee had always been somewhat impatient when it came to waiting for something to arrive. The weeks before Christmas were almost torture for her when she was a child. Anticipation and suspense made her grumpy and kept her awake at night. Waiting the ten days until Manfred arrived to free the spirits seemed like an eternity.

Finally, the day arrived; and every time the doorbell rang, she ran to see if it was Manfred. Of course, since Jeannie and Julie wanted to be there, twice she was disappointed. Manfred arrived right on time, and once again said he would have to work alone so as not to alarm the spirits. He did promise to relate any incidents to the small group afterward. He explained that through a series of chants and burning incense, the four spirits would come to him, and then he would speak a simple command to each of them. Each command would be different, but he would approach the two children together. He would be able to tell immediately if the command was followed because of their behavior. If they resisted the command, the spirits would linger and not disappear. With that, he was off to the basement first to talk to the elderly servant.

Marilee looked at Jeannie and said, "Don't laugh or it might jinx the whole procedure."

Jeannie stifled a laugh but managed to say, "It really does sound like it's too good to be true. Let's hope he gives you a money back guarantee."

"Well, I will ask what happens if they come back. Of course, we didn't know they were here, so how will we know if they are gone?"

The conversation continued for the hour and a half it took Manfred to complete his work focusing mostly on ghosts. Since it had become known to a fairly large group of friends that Marilee had a ghost in the house, people always wanted to tell about their experiences with a ghost. As a result, all three women had many stories to relate to each other.

Manfred returned to the kitchen looking the color of a ghost. This obviously was draining work. He sat down at the table and accepted the cup of tea Marilee offered. After several sips, he seemed to regain some strength.

He began with the servant release. "The elderly man was hanging around because he could not find his wife who was also a servant in the house during the war. I surmise there had been several times soldiers had come to the house, some before and some after everyone had left. On one occasion, it had been dreadful as the soldiers tried to take the male servants and make them join the militia. Of course there was resistance, and it was at that time Edward, the servant, took a spell and died. He was unsure where his wife had gone, so he was concerned for her safety. She never did return, but he was still waiting for her. Most likely, she and the other women had found a hiding spot and later left the house. I convinced him she had left but later died and was waiting for him in heaven, so he went willingly."

Manfred took a deep breath, several more sips of tea, and continued. "The other gentleman who was conscious of time was probably a guest of the family. He was staying here while waiting for some papers to arrive for the family to sign. He was a lawyer. He was always in control of every situation during his life and could not leave until his task was completed. I explained to him the papers had been signed, and the family were happy with the situation. He probably had a heart attack from worry while he waited. He was somewhat reluctant, but he did finally leave."

Again, more deep breaths and more tea, and then he said, "The children were the saddest to work with. I do believe they died during the Spanish flu epidemic. As they were young, they relied on their parents to do everything for them. I think the parents may have died of the flu as well. The children were very sad and were waiting for their parents to come and get them. Once they realized I knew where their parents were, it was easy to convince them to go."

Manfred continued to tell the group that if they noticed any strange activity other than the sobbing, it might mean the spirits came back, but he felt sure they would not be bothered. Even before they could ask, he told them he guaranteed his work and would always come back to help if they needed him.

Marilee, Jeannie, and Julie were speechless, could not think of any questions for him, or ask about the spirits. When he stood to leave, Marilee went to the office and brought back an envelope containing a cheque for his work.

"Thank you," he said and left through the back door.

No one spoke for almost five minutes, and then they all began to talk at once.

OCTOBER

October was going to seem tame after the spirit removal last month. Marilee had closed off booking so there would be rooms for the family for Thanksgiving. She had a few guest the first week, but it was an easy time. She had plenty of time for shopping and baking.

Phillip, however, was up to his ears in grapes. The picking was complete, and the grapes were now in vats fermenting. Every day, they had to be checked and punched down to allow the cap of skins to keep them moist. They also had to be aerated every day to encourage extracting the color from the skins of the red grapes and to improve the flavor. Since the vats were being stored at another facility, it meant travelling the forty-five-minute drive to and from the storage spot.

Phillip could hardly wait for next year when all this work would be done on their property. Dave and Mike were always there to work with the juice, but Phillip felt he should be involved as well.

The weather had cooperated this year, and the grape harvest had been successful, so this year held promise for excellent wine.

The work on the winery building, however, had hit a snag. Some of the building materials Phillip had chosen were back ordered and would not be available until the end of the month. The footings were poured for the work area, and the wall structure was up, but now while they waited for the custom-made roof trusses, nothing more could be done.

The old barn, which would be the tasting room, was taking shape though. The basic electrical work and plumbing was completed, and the carpenters were now constructing the cabinetry. The next few weeks should show amazing progress, and hopefully by mid-November, it would be close to finished.

Marilee had already arranged for the grand opening to be the second weekend in December. The caterer was hired, the menu was planned, and the invitations were being printed. Now they hoped this delay would not interfere with the party.

"I guess if things out in the work area are not finished, we will just not show anyone that part in December," Phillip said to Marilee as they worked on the guest list.

"People really just want to see the glamorous parts anyway," said Marilee. "We can always showcase the other part of the winery when a new release is ready as I'm sure it will be done by then."

"It better be done by then," he mumbled as he left to go back to the planning and accounting books in the office.

Marilee was happily baking in the kitchen, hoping to have most things ready for Thanksgiving when the whole family would be here for the weekend. She wanted to spend time with her grandchildren and their parents rather than in the kitchen cooking. Last year, they had enjoyed going to an antique fair, so maybe they would try that again. "I'll check on line for tickets and times," she said to herself.

The Friday night of the Thanksgiving weekend was finally here, and Marilee was looking forward to everyone's arrival by noon on Saturday. She had only heard sobbing twice in the last week at night, and it had been Hannah's soft sobbing that let you know she was still there. Marilee hoped it might be very quiet during the weekend as one of her sons-in-law was not particularly fond of the idea of a ghost in the house. Both her daughters were intrigued by the idea and liked to hear the stories Marilee told.

The other son-in-law really didn't say much about whether he liked or disliked the situation. The two boys, however, were always talking about what they would do if they saw a ghost and how brave they would be in scaring it away. Apparently, they both felt they had superhero powers when it came to chasing ghosts.

The weekend was all planned with winery visits and antique show. Last year had been a hit, so they were just repeating the same entertainment. Phillip, of course, had an added agenda of looking at details of the tasting rooms of other wineries. Marilee had the task of finding some antiques that would fit into the barn's decor. It would be easy to sleep tonight as both had been so busy the past few days getting ready for the weekend.

*   *   *

Hannah, however, had a different plan. Her senses were heightened, and she felt Peter was very close and would appear at any time. She had been keeping watch at the windows on both sides of the house to make sure she didn't miss anything. She suddenly heard the sound of gunfire. It sounded faint so was not close to the house, but it continued for quite some time. All was quiet again until Hannah heard a horse galloping on the road and getting closer and closer. She held herself tightly as she floated to various parts of the house, hoping it would be Peter and not a soldier coming to raid the house.

The galloping horse was now right at the end of their lane. She saw a dashing solitary figure wearing a cocked hat and a red coat with shiny epaulets. He was also wearing a decorative scarf that was waving behind him as he rode. "Who must he be, and where was he going," she asked herself.

Annoyed that she did not know what was happening, she proceeded to slam doors as she returned to the attic. A short time later, she heard the gunfire start again. "There must be a battle taking place close to the house," she thought.

The firing continued for a long time, and the only sound that interrupted it was the galloping of horses and marching of at least a hundred soldiers going along the road in the same direction as the lone rider.

Now Hannah was really in a state as she was worried about her father and Peter. She knew he was close but was unable to locate him. Hannah spent many hours travelling up and down the stairs, slamming doors as she went, not even being careful about being seen by anyone. "Why should I use the dumbwaiter and hide?" she said. "This is my house."

*   *   *

Marilee awoke early the next morning, not rested but quite invigorated by the dream she had. At breakfast, she relayed the scene to Phillip and said, "Hannah must have seen the soldiers and heard the gunfire from the Battle of Queenston Heights. It must have been General Brock she saw riding toward the battle from Fort George. Do you remember last year on this weekend it was the anniversary of the battle? Hannah is on the right date just 201 years behind us. Now I will know what she is seeing by the dates."

Phillip just continued to drink his coffee and eat his toast. He was interested in the ghost residing in their attic but not to the same degree as Marilee. He felt that ghost information was better left alone and not investigated.

However, he knew Marilee was fascinated by it and loved her enough to let her continue researching the family who once lived in their house. He just hoped she would not be disappointed or worse hurt by the end result, if there was an end.

The family all arrived shortly after lunch, and it was the usual confusion and noise. The three grandchildren were each now a year older and bigger, so there was more running, more noise, and more kid stuff to carry to the bedrooms.

Since it was a lovely fall day, they all decided to spend the time outside exploring around the property. There was the newly renovated barn to see and the construction site where the winery work buildings would eventually be located.

Phillip took Jonathon and Owen aside and said, "Come down to the dock with me. I have a surprise to show you."

"What is it, Grandpa? Is it a jet ski?"

Phillip laughed. "You will just have to wait till we get there." They were running now, so he had to hurry to keep up.

"It's a boat," they shrieked. "And it has our name on it. Can we go for a ride?"

Phillip laughed. He'd found a small boat just right for three people and had painted JON-OWEN on the side. There were some oars and life jackets in the boat just waiting for someone to take it out on the river.

Once the lifejackets were all done up and the boys were in the boat, Phillip stepped in carefully and pushed off from the dock. It was quite shallow and calm along the bank to the north, so Phillip showed them how to use the oars and the safe spots to paddle. He also gave them the rules about who could use the boat and when it could be taken out.

Each boy had a turn at trying to use the oars, but it would be a while before they were really proficient at it. As they returned to the dock, the rest of the family were waiting for them, and Jonathon and Owen had smiles a mile wide on their faces. Phillip looked pretty pleased as well.

The rest of the day was spent relaxing and talking. After dinner, the children were put to bed, and the adults continued to chat in the living room.

About an hour later, Jonathon came downstairs and said, "I can't sleep because of the talking."

His dad took him back up and said the adults would move to the family room so he could sleep.

"No, Dad, it's not you guys talking. It's the people behind this wall."

"This wall behind your bed?" his dad asked.

"Yes. They are whispering and singing songs like Mom used to sing to Owen when he was a baby."

Owen and Jonathon were sleeping in the room that backed onto the old part of the house. The staircase to the attic was right behind his bed. Gary knew about the ghost in the house and so did Jonathon, but he had no intention of telling Jonathon that's who might be singing.

"I will ask Grandma if she has the radio on in her office at the back. Maybe that's what you hear," Gary told Jonathon. He sat on the edge of the bed quietly rubbing Jonathon's back and listened for noises or singing but did not hear anything. After a very short time, Jonathon was asleep, and Gary crept out and went down to tell the group what Jonathon had said.

After relaying the story, no one spoke.

"This is a new development," said Marilee. "Maybe Hannah likes small children and is singing lullabies to them."

Both moms looked worried, and Emma spoke first. "I hope she doesn't wake Amanda as she doesn't go back to sleep that easily."

"Don't anyone tell Owen, or we will all be up there with capes on searching for her," said Janine.

"Just keep the doors open tonight and a light on in the hall, and I'm sure things will be fine," said Marilee, trying to reassure them. "Tell Jonathon in the morning it was my radio in the office. Maybe he has the special gift to recognize spirits like I do?"

No one made a comment.

The next morning, everyone greeted each other with a questioning look, but no one had heard anything, and Jonathon didn't seem to remember, so no explanations were given.

The men took the boys to the fort for the day, and the women and Amanda went to the antique fair. They were not able to see as much this year as Amanda, who was two and a half, wanted to walk rather than ride in the stroller. It was a slow process, but Janine managed to find a table that was perfect for her house, and Emma bought an antique rocking chair for Amanda. Marilee found several decorative items for the barn.

Later that evening, after a delicious turkey dinner, the children went to bed, and everyone hoped there would be no talking behind the walls tonight. Marilee was the last to go to bed and walked past the children's rooms to make sure all was well. As she passed the stairs to the attic, she stopped and listened but heard nothing. She said her prayer that Hannah would be quiet tonight and went to bed.

*   *   *

Hannah was in a happy mood, which wasn't always the case. She had heard children's voices and thought maybe her sister and some others were coming home. When she looked out the attic window, she saw children going for a boat ride with a man. She had seen this man before in the kitchen but didn't really understand why he wore such odd-looking clothes. The children were dressed in colored, loose fitting tops, and short pants that were a combination of several colors going perpendicular to each other. "Quite odd," she thought to herself.

She was worried about them being on the river in case the soldiers came, but she watched until the boat was back at the dock, and everyone returned safely to the house. She saw three children—two young boys and a small girl. Hannah loved children. She knew it was not her sister, but she was happy the house once again had children playing in it.

Hannah watched carefully from a hiding spot in a closet where the two boys were getting ready for bed. They certainly seemed to have a lot of energy and had lots to say to the adults, even arguing sometimes about things the parents wanted them to do. Her parents would never have allowed her or her sister and brother to talk like that to adults.

Watching while the parents read stories to them and listening to the chitchat after the parents left made Hannah a bit sad. To cheer herself up, she decided to sing a song that her mother had often sung to her when she was small.

Baby, baby, go to sleep,
The stars are shining bright,
Angels will watch you sleeping,
All through the night.

The one little boy fell asleep, but the other was looking around the room from his bed. Suddenly, he got out of bed and left the room. "Why did he leave? Did he not like my song?" Soon he returned with a grownup that stayed until he was asleep. Hannah decided to return to the attic and watch through her window in the hope of seeing Peter. She would return the next night to sing to the children.

This didn't happen, though, because Hannah forgot about the children as there were soldiers on the road again. This time, there were several soldiers with a horse pulling a cart. There was a body lying in the back of the cart covered with a blanket. Someone must have died during all the fighting she heard several days ago. He must be important because there was only one body, and there certainly had been a lot of gunfire. It was all very puzzling and not what Hannah wanted to see. She knew Peter was around somewhere close, but she could not see him. She wished she could go outside.

Only once had she been able to go outside the house and see her mother reach her uncle's farm. Now every time she tried to go out, something was in the way and blocked her exit. Frustrated, Hannah went back to the attic, slammed the door, and sat by the window watching the river.

*   *   *

Marilee related her dream to Phillip the next morning, and they decided it would be better not to tell the family. If no one mentioned any noises, it would just remain their secret. That was the case, and the morning was filled with gathering all their toys and packing for the ride home. The boys did convince Grandpa that there was time for one more ride in the new boat. It had been a great Thanksgiving.

Guests coming to the B&B were fewer now as late fall approached. Marilee enjoyed this time of year as it gave her time to get involved in other interests and local events. She decided she needed to research more about Peter. The time factor did not seem to be right for Peter to marry Hannah's younger sister. Couples did get married at much younger ages then, but Marilee figured Hannah's sister Mary was at least five years younger.

The rest of the week looked like she could spend some time at the museum going through documents, but today, she had some organizing to do for the opening of the tasting barn in December.

All the decorative aspects were awaiting installation while the contractors finished the electrical work. The next thing to happen would be putting up all the lights. This would give the place a distinctive look as the painting was finished. After that, the final floors would be laid. Marilee was excited because then she could start bringing in the furniture and adding the finishing decorative touches. She hoped the barn would be ready about two weeks before the grand opening so glasses and extra tables and chairs could arrive prior to the party day.

Marilee and Phillip had decided to call the tasting room "the Barn" rather than give it a fancy name. Since it had been an actual barn, the name seemed appropriate.

Marilee was walking out to the barn when she saw Phillip talking to some men at the back of the barn. She had seen the landscaper's truck drive in earlier so assumed it was them. As she approached, she heard part of the conversation.

"I'm not sure what we have hit, but the men stopped digging as soon as their shovel hit something," said the boss. "Do you know if there are pipes here for gas or water? No one had the utility companies come to map them out for us, so we can't continue until we know."

Phillip said, "All the pipes are at the other side and are right beside the walkway. The markings were here earlier but have worn off. You are safe to dig here, and there is no plan for any landscaping where the utilities are as the gravel is already down in that spot."

"I hope you are right as I don't want anyone getting hurt."

Phillip knew he was right about the location but could understand about the safety aspect as well. He then told the landscaper he could bring in someone to mark it if it made them feel safer. He really didn't want to, though, as days would be lost as well as dollars. The men agreed to continue with just Phillip's word. The truck loaded with all the shrubs and trees was already sitting on the property as were the crew to do the work. If all went according to plan, the landscaping would be done this week. One more job to cross off the list.

Phillip and Marilee wanted to see what the men had run into, though, so they followed the workers back to where they had been digging. "We might want to be careful digging here, even though we know it's not utilities," said Phillip.

While everyone watched, one of the workers carefully scraped away the soil beside the barn wall. There was a scraping noise that sounded like more pottery. Soon, pieces of fabric could be seen covering something bulky. Phillip bent over and carefully lifted whatever was wrapped up from the hole. The crowd was silently watching as he peeled away the dirty layers of partially rotted fabric to expose two pewter candlesticks.

"How long have these been here?" asked Marilee. "Do you think they belonged to the Van Everys?"

"Possibly," answered Phillip. "I wonder if there is more stuff buried. Dig carefully along this side of the barn. If there is more, it's likely to be buried at the same depth," he said to the crew. He then carried the candlesticks to the house to clean them and see if there were any markings to date them.

By the end of the morning, the landscapers had found a china platter, some bits of old moldy lace, several teaspoons, and a wooden music box. The music box and the lace had not survived well in the ground, but the other pieces were in one piece, just dirty.

"I will leave this mystery for you to solve, Marilee. If they are valuable and belonged to the original owners, we could find them a place of honor in the tasting barn," said Phillip.

Marilee managed to find two days to do some research at the museum. She discovered the name of Peter Gillham and found some property deeds with his name on them. The properties, however, were not on the river and quite a distance away from the Van Every house and the land owned by Peter's father. Also, the date seemed to be too early for Peter to have lived on the newly discovered farm. The land had been granted to a Peter Gillham before the war started, and he was married at that time to a girl named Mary.

"This generation were not too original in naming their children as most of them were named for brothers or aunts," said Marilee to the girl at the desk. "It makes it difficult to really sort out all the generations."

"I know." The receptionist continued, "In order to really sort the town out, we had to develop a form to keep it all straight. I can give you a blank form to use to keep the two families organized by date rather than just name."

"That would probably help a lot," said Marilee.

"Also, you may want to reference some of the church records to check for marriages and baptisms. Though there aren't prior to 1813 as they were burned with the town."

Marilee had planned on doing that sometime; she just hadn't found the time yet. "Thanks. I think I will but not until next week."

She took the form and all her notes and headed home. Maybe putting everything out on a large table would help her organize this complicated family. She also knew she had to reread the letters to see if she had missed anything, and since the copies were at the museum, she would have to retrieve the originals again from Hannah's doll. She wasn't sure it was a wise thing to do, but it seemed she had no other choice.

NOVEMBER

The weekend was over; there were now no guests until December, and all the planning for the party at the barn was completed as much as it could be. Marilee thought about asking Jeannie to come over and help but decided she just wanted to get this step done today.

She climbed the stairs to the attic, opened the door, and as she entered, she said, "Hello, Hannah. It's just me, Marilee. I need to read your letters again."

She hoped if she announced who she was and what she wanted, Hannah would not be angry. There was no answer of course and no other sign, so Marilee went to the trunk and opened it. The doll was still there wrapped in the clothes, just as she had left it. Marilee thought Hannah maybe wasn't interested in the doll anymore, so she decided to take it downstairs to read the letters. She removed the clothes wrapped around the doll, put the clothes back in the trunk, and closed the lid. She quickly left the attic and returned downstairs.

"Why am I so nervous about being up there now?" she asked herself as she walked to their bedroom. Once there, she carefully unstitched the neck and removed the letters. Marilee decided not to restitch the neck now as she would do it when she returned the letters. She might just make another copy so she would have one with all her research notes. She placed the doll on the rocking chair with its head propped against a cushion and went downstairs.

Marilee had taken over the dining room table to spread out all her research notes, so she took the letters down there to keep everything together. She sat down and began to read the letters found last year inside the doll and in the dumbwaiter.

Rereading them was as exciting as discovering the information the first time. The next thing she heard was Phillip calling her. When she looked at her watch, she saw it was 2:00 p.m.

"Have you had lunch yet?" Phillip asked when he found her in the dining room.

"No, I have been rereading these letters in the doll. I guess we need to eat lunch. Have you eaten yet?"

"No. I was busy with the architects for the building, and we wanted to finish up some details today so the next step can begin."

"Well, let's have lunch," said Marilee, forgetting she was going to make a copy of the letters so she could return these to the doll.

The rest of the day was a series of interruptions requiring Marilee to make several phone calls and follow up on work that was to be done for the winery. Maybe tomorrow she could get back to the letters. That night in bed, she was going over in her head all the unfinished things that she started during the day, but she seemed to just keep repeating the same items again and again.

* * *

Hannah was sitting at the window when she heard footsteps on the stairs. She decided to stay very quiet and see who was coming to the attic. If need be, she could begin screaming in her high-pitched scream to scare them.

The door opened, and the woman from downstairs was coming into the room. Suddenly, the woman spoke and called her by name. Hannah watched her carefully as she walked toward the trunk, opened it and picked up the doll, and removed the fabric wrapped around it. Now she was really concerned. The woman then returned the old clothes, shut the trunk, and turned to leave the attic.

"Why is she taking my doll, and how does she know my name?" Hannah was speaking to herself, but she was totally puzzled. She didn't know why the woman needed to read the letters either. Hannah decided to follow her downstairs to see what she was going to do. She had never done this before, but somehow the woman seemed kind and not a threat, even though she was taking the doll.

Hannah watched with fear as Marilee unpicked the stitches and removed the letters. When Marilee left her bedroom to go downstairs, Hannah stayed in the room and went to her doll. How sad she looked with her neck unstitched and her head flopping to one side. The sewing kit was on the floor beside the rocking chair, so Hannah looked for a needle, and when she found just the right size, she restitched the neck of her doll. She held the doll close to her for a while and then put it back on the chair. She suddenly noticed, though, that her doll looked so worn and tattered. The clothes had some holes in them and dirt in places.

"How did it get like that?" she asked herself. "I took such good care of my doll. I will leave my doll here tonight until that lady puts the letters back, and then I will take her back to the attic with me. Tomorrow, I will go back down and bring her up here with me."

Hannah gave her doll another hug and sat her on the chair. She then floated back up to the attic to watch for Peter. It was sad being alone in the attic, and now her doll was not with her either. Hannah spent the rest of the night sobbing while sitting at the window.

*   *   *

Marilee had heard the sobbing all night and hoped it was not because she had taken the doll from the attic. After breakfast, she quickly made some copies of the letters on her printer and went back to the bedroom to return them to the doll. When she picked the doll up from the rocking chair, a sudden chill came over her. She knew she hadn't restitched the doll's neck, but the piece of yarn she had taken out was now stitched across the neck, and the ribbon was covering the spot. Marilee was worried that she might be doing things in her sleep but knew she could never do that.

Just then, she felt a cold feeling on her one leg. She reached down to brush at it, but it kept bothering her. It was like there was a wet cloth being dragged across her leg under her jeans. Could it be Hannah was in the room watching her? Not wanting to scare her, Marilee sat in the rocking chair and held the doll close and rocked it as you would a child. The cold feeling on her leg stopped. Marilee then carefully removed the ribbon necklace and began to take out the stitches in the neck. As she did this, she began talking to Hannah, telling her everything she was doing.

"Hannah, I am going to put the letters back inside the doll for safekeeping. Then I will sew her neck back up and take her back to the attic to be with you. I need the letters to find out more about Peter. If I can find out more about him, I may be able to find out where he went."

At the mention of Peter's name, Hannah became very excited and began almost flying around the room.

Marilee noticed the curtains on the window were blowing as if a wind was coming in the window. "Could Hannah be in the room now and hearing her?" Marilee asked herself. If so, this was a first. Marilee had never communicated with a spirit before. "I must keep talking to her, so she knows I am her friend," she thought. If Hannah knows what I am doing, she may stay around and let us know she is here.

When Marilee finished repairing the doll, she took it back to the attic all the while, explaining each action to Hannah. She wanted Hannah to stay and listen to her. Hopefully someday, Hannah might reveal herself to Marilee, although Marilee wasn't really sure what she would do if she saw Hannah.

Marilee left the attic and returned to the kitchen. She really needed another cup of coffee and a bit of time to take this in. Being able to detect Hannah's presence in the room was a new development. She knew she couldn't tell anybody about this yet, but she wanted to. She was also thinking of all the questions she wanted to ask Hannah the next time she realized they were together in a room. The big question was what rooms could Hannah go to, and where did she stay most of the time? Marilee had thought she stayed in the attic, but now it seemed the master bedroom and the upstairs hall way were also on the list.

Marilee went to the office and picked up the copied letters and returned to the kitchen. She began to reread them to see if there were any clues as to where Peter may have ended up. Unfortunately, the information in the letters did not give her any further clues that might help figure out where Peter went. She was no further ahead in finding out where Peter might have gone or who he had married. She was going to have to go into town to look at old records at the church.

Marilee decided to do this on her own because she knew she would end up telling Jeannie about feeling Hannah's presence if they went together. She would tell no one, not even Phillip until she either heard Hannah talk or saw her in a room.

Marilee packed up all her research notes and drove into town to the church in hopes of finding someone there that could help her. When she arrived, the door was open, and several parishioners were standing in the entrance chatting.

One gentleman turned and asked, "Can we help you?"

Marilee explained who and what she was looking for, and to her surprise, two people offered to help. They took her to a room packed with folders and papers and files with papers. How anyone could find anything in this room? Marilee wondered. One of the gentlemen immediately went to a corner, lifted a box, and took out four very fat files.

"These might be a good place to start," he said to Marilee.

"I'm glad you are here to help me, or I would not have any idea where to begin," said Marilee.

"I am the one who put most of this paperwork in this room," he said. "I may be the only one who knows."

Marilee was glad he had been at the door when she arrived and took the files to the empty desk and began to open them. The gentleman introduced himself as John and asked a few more questions about what she was looking for. He said he knew a bit about the Blacks in Niagara and suggested she start with the last file.

Marilee thought John might be the answer to more than one research question, so she told him she was searching for information about Peter Gillham and his family. John got up from his chair and walked to another part of the room and pulled out a few more files. She wanted to ask if they had beds here because at this rate, she might be here for several days going through all these files.

Marilee began going through the files systematically and found the names of property owners on the river. Not only did it have the original owners but also all the subsequent owners right up to 1900.

After about an hour, she came across the Gillham name and noticed the property first changed ownership in 1815. That was interesting as the war was over by then, but Peter's parents had left to go across the river three years before that.

The new owner was not anyone named Gillham but a James Durham. The name seemed familiar, and Marilee thought she had seen the name before, but it was not one that factored into the hunt for Peter. She jotted the name down into her notes in case she came across it again.

She continued going through the files but didn't find any names of significance. It was disappointing not to find something, so Marilee thought she would have to take a different path to find something. She decided to look in the other files to try to find out some information about Joseph.

It wasn't long before she came across the name Joseph Jackson and then found several addresses for him. His original address was the same as listed for the Van Every farm. This must be the farmworker who had delivered the notes for Hannah and Peter and the same who had been left on the farm when the family left during the war.

The notes were interesting as they did not just give names and addresses but included some anecdotal notes about the individuals. They described Joseph as a loyal worker on the Van Every farm who later joined the Colored Corps and fought for the British during the War of 1812. He later married, purchased some land in the town, built a house, and raised his family. The records as far as 1900 stated his descendents lived in the area.

"Well," thought Marilee, "at least I have found out something worthwhile today." Just then, John came back to see how she was doing.

"I seem to be running into roadblocks all the time when it comes to the Gillham family," she said.

"Many of the families moved away from the river as the properties became expensive and were often considered to be vulnerable to attacks from across the river," said John. "You might want to try looking at areas that were settled after 1814 and further inland."

As he was talking, John walked over to another table in the room and picked up another stack of files. "These might prove to be more worthwhile."

"Thanks," said Marilee. "I think I may have to come back another day as I don't want to keep you too long."

"Don't worry about those of us who spend all our time here. We love it, and our wives are thrilled to have us out of the house for a few hours. I will be here the next two afternoons after 1:00 p.m., so if you want to drop in, please do."

"I could come on Friday," said Marilee.

"I look forward to helping you then."

Marilee helped John close up some of the files she had used and kept track of where he put the new ones she would look through the next time and then left the small basement room and made her way up the stairs to daylight. This had been a somewhat successful day, and maybe Friday would be even more fulfilling. John had become her new best friend.

Marilee was anxious for Friday to arrive when she could begin her search again for news of either Peter or Joseph, but first, she had some details for the Christmas party and opening of the tasting room to complete.

Today, she would be out running errands and picking up needed supplies for the party. Jeannie had agreed to help her, and Marilee was grateful as she was a very efficient friend. They were meeting back at the house at four to check what was left on the list.

Marilee finished all her jobs by three and returned home. After carrying all the supplies into the house, she decided some tea would hit the spot. As she walked into the pantry to get the tea, she was astounded to see a brick from the wall on the floor. Her first thoughts were that the house was falling apart, but then she worried that a critter, like a squirrel or mouse, might have tried to get into the house.

Just then, the back door opened, and Jeannie called out, "Hi, it's just me with bags of goodies for the party."

Marilee jumped at the sound of a voice but was glad someone was here to help discover how this happened. "I'm in the pantry. You need to see this."

Jeannie came to the pantry and at first did not see the brick on the floor, but when she did, the first words out of her mouth were "how did that get there?"

"I found it like that when I came in here a few minutes ago. I know it wasn't like that when I left this morning. Was there an earthquake that I didn't hear about, and if so, why isn't there more damage?"

"No earthquakes. It must have been loose and fallen out maybe when a door was slammed."

Marilee and Jeannie moved forward and peered into the space where the brick had been. Both gasped at the same time, and Jeannie reached in and pulled out a several sheets of paper all folded individually.

"I'm making tea, and we are going to read these in the kitchen," said Marilee.

Jeannie followed her into the kitchen, clutching the papers. Even though she had not opened it up, she could tell there was writing on the other side of one of the sheets.

"Do you suppose this was a hiding place for letters during the war?" Marilee asked while she was making tea. "Maybe Hannah or her parents put it there. We did find the ones in the dumbwaiter last year that were written by Peter, but I thought that was it."

"Did you ever notice a loose brick in the pantry before?"

"Not really, but I wasn't usually looking for anything like that when I went into the pantry," replied Marilee.

The tea was made, and both Jeannie and Marilee sat at the table and carefully unfolded the first letter. The writing was smudged as though it had been wet at some point, but fortunately the words, though faint, could still be read. Silence enveloped the room as the women read the letter.

Marilee spoke first. "This tells us what happened to Joseph and where he went during the war. Now that we know who he fought with, we can find out more about him through military records. I did have a dream one night where Hannah saw Joseph come back to the house, but I missed the part about the letter. I do believe that Hannah put this letter here for safekeeping. Let's look at the next one."

The next piece of paper was a list of items with the words *Behind the Barn* written at the bottom. "These sound like the items that were dug up when the workers were landscaping around the tasting barn," exclaimed Marilee." Hannah's mother must have made a list and put it here so she would remember where she buried them. But you would think she would have dug them up once she came back after the war. Unless—"

"She never returned because she either died, or the whole family was killed in the war," interrupted Jeannie. "No wonder Hannah is so upset."

"Wow. This makes a lot more things to find out now about the Van Every family. For every piece of information I discover, there are at least three more questions that come up. This is going to take forever."

Marilee thought about telling Jeannie about realizing Hannah had been in the bedroom while she was there but decided to wait until she had a bit more evidence and maybe more answers.

Marilee and Jeannie then opened the third paper and found a letter from Mr. Van Every that had been written sometime during the war when he had returned to the house. It was written to his wife telling her about the terrible conditions for the soldiers and how he hoped to see her soon. There was no date on it, so it was impossible to tell when it had been written.

"I don't think Mrs. Van Every saw this letter as she would have kept it somewhere else," said Marilee. "This letter sort of confirms she never returned to this farm after the war. It may be hard to find out what happened as women did not own property, and if she stayed at William's farm, she would not be listed anywhere."

Marilee and Jeannie talked about the Van Every family and Hannah and Joseph for a while and then realized time was slipping by, and they had totally forgotten about planning the party.

The next hour was spent crossing things off lists and adding more items to the to-do list. There was two weeks left until the party, but most of the big jobs were either completed or assigned to someone else. Next week, they would be able to see the completed party room in the tasting barn and then begin putting everything in its place.

Dates were written into appointment books, and Marilee and Jeannie planned to meet in a week. Marilee did invite Jeannie to go with her to the church library on Friday to see if they could find more information about Joseph.

Marilee took the letters into her office and put them in the folder with the copies of Hannah's letters. She then returned to the pantry to check out how far in this hole behind the brick went. It really was only a bit deeper than the depth of the brick, and as there was a wall behind the space, she decided not to worry about critters and replaced the brick. She made a mental note as to where it was as she wanted to show Phillip.

Next week was the beginning of December, and Marilee had not thought about Christmas, decorating, or presents. She decided this Friday would be the last researching she could do until she was ready for Christmas.

DECEMBER

It had been quiet in the attic lately, so Hannah must be busy thinking or happy just watching. Marilee was worried about the next weekend, though, as it was the anniversary of the burning of the town when the American soldiers left. She had guests arriving for the weekend, and she suspected Hannah might become emotional again during this anniversary, but as she seemed to running a year behind, things might be OK. For the moment, though, she would enjoy the peaceful nights and get as much sleep as she could.

Marilee met Jeannie at the church shortly after ten, and they descended to the basement. John was there to help them find the files again.

"Are there any files about the sale of farms after the war?" asked Marilee. "I am especially interested in ones along the river. Also, were there any other Van Everys listed as land owners in the area but not on the river?"

"We do have records of farms changing hands along the river and in other areas," said John. "Our original maps of the area would reveal all the land grants to men in the area. That might help you."

John then walked to the other side of the room and without any hesitation picked up three files and brought them to Marilee and Jeannie. "Try looking in these. I will be upstairs so just come and call me if you need anything else."

After he left, Marilee said to Jeannie, "He must have photographic memory to know what is in each of these folders and where he puts them."

"I wouldn't dare put anything back on one of these piles for fear of placing it in the wrong spot," said Jeannie.

They began looking through the files and at first chatted a bit about what they hoped to find, but soon, it was very quiet as they were both totally engrossed in their work. Jeannie spoke first and said, "This property chart shows that the farm next to the Van Every's was owned by a James Durham. There is no mention of Gillhams at all. There is also a farm two concessions over listed as being owned by a Peter Gillham. The date on this document is 1817. It also states that the Van Every farm which was lot 10 was now owned by a man named Vrooman. He also owns the one to the North. Didn't he always own the one next to Van Every's?"

"He did. Lot 10 must have been sold to Vrooman after the war. Now I am curious as to why it was sold. I think we have to look up dates when some of the Van Everys died. They apparently attended this church, so the records should be here or with military information if David Van Every was killed during the war."

"One thing just leads to the next, doesn't it? Are you finding anything of interest, Marilee?"

Marilee didn't answer right away but eventually said, "I have found a William and a Samuel Van Every who were also deeded property in the area about the same time as Hannah's father. William's farm would have been within walking distance and farther from the fighting. Samuel's land was closer to town so maybe not as safe. William eventually owned four blocks of land around his original holding, so that seems the logical spot for Sarah Van Every to go."

John returned to the basement at that point to let them know the church was closing in ten minutes. "Have you been successful in finding what you were looking for?"

"Yes and no," answered Marilee. "Now we need to look at dates people died to see if our hunches are right. Do you have records of dates people died during the war and after?"

"Only after the war, and even then, there are several years missing. As you know, the town was burned in 1813, and before that, for a period, it was used as a hospital. We can certainly try to find them for you. I will be here on Tuesday and Thursday next week if you want some help."

Marilee decided she didn't want to have to explain all the details over again to a new person, so she said, "We could come in on Tuesday afternoon if that works for you, John."

"It's a date then. I will just put these files back and have some more ready for you on Tuesday."

"Thank you so much," said Marilee.

As they were leaving the church, Jeannie said, "I thought you weren't going to do any more research until after Christmas."

"This is so addictive. I just have to find out the death dates so I can think about it while I am decorating the house."

They both laughed and agreed to meet on Tuesday afternoon to find out more about the Van Every and Gillham families.

At dinner that night, Marilee remarked to Phillip, "I think we are close to finding out more details about the two families. We are doing one more day of research before next weekend, and then I can concentrate on the party details. I will have some time to put up some decorations here in the house tomorrow and the next day, so I was wondering if you could bring the boxes up to the living room."

"Should I carry them up or try to use the dumbwaiter like we did last year?"

They both laughed, recalling the almost disaster when the rope broke and dropped everything down to the basement again.

"The good news was finding the letter," said Marilee.

"And here you are still searching for more letters a year later, but that's OK because you are having fun. You are having fun, aren't you?" asked Phillip.

Marilee just laughed.

That night just before she fell asleep, she went over all the details about Hannah that she could remember. She knew she shouldn't as this often led to her dreaming about the family, and tonight, it happened again.

*   *   *

Hannah had taken to wandering around the house in the dark lately. She knew at night she was less likely to bump into a strangely dressed person. She also discovered she could go into every room, but it was odd that sometimes the house was just as she remembered it, except her family was gone. At other times, it was a bright house with new-looking furniture and many pieces of unfamiliar equipment. At first, she never knew what house she would find; but after some time, she discovered if she was feeling sad and missing her mother, it was the familiar home she saw. If, however, she was just being curious and poking around for no reason, it was the new house she saw.

"I may be getting better at this ghost thing," she said to herself.

That thought made her sad, and she began to miss her family. More than anything, she wanted to have the power to leave the house and see where her mother and brother and sister were staying. She still was unable to adjust her feelings so she could leave the house.

Tonight, she stood at the front window looking west. Suddenly, she could see her mother with Elizabeth and the children all together in a small room.

"This must be my uncle's farm where they are staying," she thought. "If I am quiet and watch, maybe I can find out what is happening."

Mrs. Van Every was drying dishes as Elizabeth washed. They were discussing the meals for the next day. There were a lot of root vegetables in the garden so it would be a vegetable stew with leftover meat broth. Their days were filled with everyday tasks such as baking bread, cooking, and cleaning, but much of their time was also spent keeping the children occupied and close to the cabin. Normally, the children would be more independent and allowed to wander about the property together, but there were soldiers and natives wandering in the area, hungry and not always friendly.

William helped his uncle in the barn with the animals and spent most of his time following Uncle William around. He was not allowed to go hunting in the woods with him though.

The farm seemed like a tranquil place away from the perils of war, and it was a safe distance from the fighting. The war, however, was always on their minds, and the safety of Mr. Van Every was mentioned nightly in their prayers. No one had heard from David Van Every since he left with the British militia several months ago. Sarah mentioned to Elizabeth in her conversation about the pact she and David had made the night he left.

"We both agreed that if either of us returned to the house, we would leave a note and hide it in the loose brick in the pantry," said Sarah. "When I return, that is the first place I shall go to see if David left a note. We haven't heard any gunfire lately, so I don't know if this horrid war is over or if they are fighting farther away. We are so thankful you and William have allowed us to stay here with you, and I do not know how we will ever be able to repay your kindness."

Elizabeth turned and hugged Sarah and said, "You have sacrificed so much during this war. Having to leave your home and endure the sadness of losing Hannah has taken its toll on your family. There is sadness in your eyes and the children's. This is the least we can do. We are all family, and we must stay together and be safe until all this trouble is past."

The youngest children had stopped playing and were quietly watching their mothers hugging as if they sensed something was wrong. Sarah turned away so they would not see the tears in her eyes.

As Hannah watched this scene, she also became very sad and began to sob. As she climbed back up to the attic, the sobbing became louder and continued throughout the night.

*   *   *

The next few days, Loyalist House was a beehive of activity. There would be guests arriving for the weekend and the grand opening of the Barn was only a week away. Marilee thought she was organized but realized, while she made another list of things to do, she would need every day to be ready for guests and a party. First, she called the church office to let them know she would not be able to come in to research the families on Tuesday, and then she called Jeannie to let her know. She knew that conversation would be a long one, not only because Jeannie was helping with the party but also because she would have to tell her about the dream.

Today, she would prepare for the weekend, and then she could think about the party. It took two days, but Marilee managed to have all her Christmas decorations in place and the menus set for the weekend. Now she could start cooking for the weekend and the party.

The weekend arrived, the guests checked in, everyone was thrilled with breakfast, and best of all, Hannah kept her sobbing to a minimum, and not a single guest seemed to notice. This was the weekend of the annual Christmas House tour, and Marilee was pleased that she and Jeannie were able to see all the decorated houses in one afternoon.

Monday morning, Phillip asked Marilee to meet with the partners and the decorator early in the week so things could be finalized. Marilee now had to move into high gear as she didn't want to be the one person in the group not ready. She had a day to complete all the work. As soon as Phillip left, she called Jeannie.

"We need to spend the whole day together so we can have everything done by tomorrow afternoon."

Jeannie, in her calmest voice, said, "Marilee, it will all be done on time. I will be over in an hour with all the purchases I have made, and we can put it all together. I will meet you in the Barn. Stop worrying."

Marilee went out to the garage and got the wagon to carry everything to the Barn. It took her two trips, and she was just unloading the last few things when Jeannie appeared.

"Oh good, I can use that wagon to unload my car."

It took three trips for Jeannie to carry her purchases to the Barn, but Marilee and Jeannie were ready to begin the set up. The two friends enjoyed working together, and this was a real treat as it was a new situation, and at the end, there would be a party for all to celebrate the opening of the new winery.

At six that evening, Phillip walked into the Barn to see why the lights were still on. He stopped at the door and just stood there for a moment with his mouth open. The transformation from a finished but undecorated room to a sophisticated, modern, but welcoming tasting room was amazing. It was almost complete, and Marilee and Jeannie took a moment to see the final look. They were quite pleased with their work and wanted to finish tonight but realized that they were suddenly exhausted.

"We can finish this by noon tomorrow at the latest," said Jeannie.

"Come up to the house for dinner. I have ordered in some food and called Ralph to come over," said Phillip.

Marilee and Jeannie pushed boxes to the center of the room and just left everything else until tomorrow. They both suddenly realized they had never got around to stopping for lunch and were now starving. They hurried to the house to find a wonderful aroma and dinner waiting on the table.

Ralph and Phillip were enjoying a glass of wine while they waited. The women were quiet for the first ten minutes while they ate some dinner and then joined in the conversation. Dinner didn't last long, though, as Jeannie and Marilee quickly cleared the table, and Jeannie said to Ralph they needed to get home as tomorrow was another busy day.

As Marilee prepared for bed, she said her quiet prayer to Hannah for peace through the night. Tonight, her prayers were answered.

The Barn was ready for a party. The room was decorated, and the food was all in its place. Marilee and Phillip had an hour left until the guests would begin to arrive for the grand opening. They were all dressed and waiting for Dave, Mike, and Julie to arrive at the Barn.

"I didn't think an opening would be so nerve wracking," Phillip said to Marilee quietly. "I know we sent invitations out to all the wineries in the area, and I did get most RSVPs back, but what if more come than said, and we run out of food?"

"We will be just fine," said Marilee. "Now stop worrying. Here come Dave and Mike and Julie."

The partners were amazed at how well the room had turned out and were off with Phillip in a flash to check out the back rooms before other guests arrived.

Julie whispered to Marilee, "This is a big night for everybody. I heard at the bakeshop today some locals talking about the opening. They must be coming as they were commenting on Fox Hollow being annoyed at how fast the winery was set up and would be looking for any shortcuts that were not to code."

"They did not RSVP that they were coming, and they better not cause any trouble," Marilee added. "When Jeannie gets here, we will fill her in on the details and keep our ears open for any uncomplimentary comments. They are already spreading rumors about Hannah."

There was no time for further chatting as the guests started to arrive. It was a constant stream of people coming in. Everyone was very complimentary about what had been done to the old barn. The caterer had excelled with the food pairings, and of course, the wine was excellent.

Marilee noticed about an hour into the party, the two partners from Fox Hollow arrived, looked around, and then began what looked like an inspection of outlets, plumbing, and structure of the room. Julie found Marilee and said, "Someone needs to follow those two around in case they disappear into the back."

Just then, Mike joined them, and he said he would be happy to give them the tour. They didn't look too pleased when he joined their small group, but they couldn't very well tell him to leave them alone.

"I could show you the back room where we stock the wine and store this season's bottles," he said politely.

"No, we've seen that kind of stuff before, and anyway, we just want to know where the ghost hangs out," said one of the men in a loud voice.

"Well," said Mike calmly, "you are out of luck as there is no ghost here at the Barn. I guess you guys are fortunate you have coyotes all around your property as their howling scares any ghosts away. That woods you have at the north edge must be a haven for those critters."

It was a well-known fact that Fox Hollow did have more coyotes on their acreage than anybody else. There used to be foxes, but the coyotes had moved in and killed most of the foxes in the past few years.

Gunshots were often heard coming from the woods, but no one would admit to shooting coyotes. The town was against killing them and so were most of the locals, so Fox Hollow tried to keep it quiet.

Mike had seen one of the owners walking out of the woods one day with his gun and dragging a coyote-looking carcass. He had stopped and taken a picture with his cell phone but had done nothing with it. The owner knew this and did not want it publicized in town.

The two owners didn't speak but turned quickly and walked to the front door. Mike decided to follow them and make sure they went directly to their car. When he knew they were off the property, Mike returned to the party smiling broadly as he entered the front door. "I'll tell you later," he said to Phillip as he walked by toward the bar.

The party turned out to be a success. The speeches were just the right length, the photos of everyone were taken, and people continued to enjoy themselves. It was almost midnight when the last guests left. The best part was the catering staff had the glasses and plates all boxed ready to take with them and the leftover food packaged for Marilee to take to the house.

"I like this way of throwing a party when there are no dishes to do at the end," said Marilee.

"I agree," said Julie.

They all agreed it had been a success, and now everyone knew that Loyalist House Winery was open for business. Mike relayed his story of the Fox Hollow duo, and they all felt it would be prudent to keep an eye on them.

Everyone went home tired but happy. Marilee was so tired she crawled into bed and didn't think to say her small prayer for peace tonight.

*   *   *

Hannah was sitting by the window watching for Peter. She kept hoping he would return. She could sense he was close by, but she didn't know where. She noticed a light flicker by the river's edge and sat up straight. She watched and saw it again. It was a single light, so it must not be a group of soldiers. The light was coming closer to the house. Hannah quickly floated down to the kitchen and stood inside the pantry door. The back door opened, and even though it was dark, Hannah knew it was Peter. He had returned to her.

Of course she then remembered he was unable to see her. She must create a disturbance so he would notice. She began to fly around the room screaming in her high-pitched voice. He did not notice. Then she began to slam doors. He still did not notice. Frustrated, she purposely flew through him, but he just smoothed his hair. What was wrong with him?

Peter had decided to go into the Van Every house to see if he could find out where they all went. He knew Mr. Van Every had joined the militia, but where had the family gone? There were still personal and household items on the shelves and in the cupboards, so they must be coming back. There was evidence of some looting and destructiveness as various crockery pieces were smashed on the floor. That meant they likely had not gone far.

He walked through most of the rooms in the house but did not seem to find what he was looking for. When he entered the pantry, he ran his hand along the wall to help guide his way in the dark. His hand suddenly seemed to move part of the wall. He held up the lantern and discovered the loose brick. He pulled it out and carefully put his hand in. The letters were right near the back, and he brought them out to look at.

Peter had learned to read but had not practiced much lately, so it took him a while to go through all the letters. He was reading the last note Mrs. Van Every had written before she left and finally discovered where they had gone. He must go there as he had a plan in his mind and need to talk to Hannah's mother. He was not sure how well he would be received as they might still hold him responsible for Hannah's death. Still, he would go.

Meanwhile, Hannah had been sitting on the floor beside Peter the whole time he was reading. She knew what he was going to do next and was quite annoyed that he had not sensed that she was present and not even tried to call her. Did he not know she was still in the house?

Peter then put the letters back into the hiding place and replaced the brick, so it was even with all the others. He picked up his lantern and walked toward the back door.

Hannah was furious. She must attract his attention somehow. Before she could think up a sure way of doing this, he opened the door and left. She watched him go back down to the river and disappear along the shore toward the Gillham farm. She must find a way to go to the Gillham farm somehow. Right now, she was devastated and just returned to the attic, picked up her doll and cried as loud as she could, and continued to do so until it was daylight.

*   *   *

Marilee could hear the crying in her dream but never really woke up fully until just before dawn. She knew she was fully awake now, but she could still hear the crying. This was a new development she thought. She didn't know if she should go up to the attic or just ignore it. She finally decided to put on her housecoat and go up to the attic and see if there was any way she could console Hannah.

She opened the attic door and began to climb the stairs. She would leave the door open so Phillip would figure out where she was. The crying softened a bit and was more of a sob now. When she entered the room, she saw the doll leaning against nothing on the window seat.

"Hannah must be sitting in the window," she said to herself. Marilee sat in the rocking chair and did not speak for a while. The sobbing had stopped.

Marilee decided if she spoke to Hannah, it might help. "Hannah, I know you saw Peter tonight." The doll moved slightly. "Was Peter here in your house last night? If he was, just shake your dolls head up and down to say yes and sideways for no."

The dolls head did not move, and then suddenly, the whole doll moved in an up-and-down motion.

"Did Peter see you?"

Again, nothing and then a sideways motion.

"You must be sad that he was unable to see you. Sometimes people in the real world are not able to see those in the spirit world as they do not understand that you are still here. It might take time for Peter to realize you are still here. Be patient Hannah and keep watching for him. I think eventually he will know you are here. He just needs time."

Marilee didn't know why she said those words or if they would help, but the sobbing had stopped, and the doll was not moving. She then saw the doll fall to the window ledge and noticed a breeze near her legs. Marilee steeled herself to not move, although she wasn't sure she could even if she had to. This was an unreal situation.

The doll then moved and again seemed to be leaning on thin air by the window. Hannah must be sitting there watching again.

"I may have just been hugged by a ghost," she said to herself. "I must go back downstairs now, but I will come to visit again," Marilee said in the direction of the window.

She then walked slowly to the stairs and turned and took one last look at the window. She wasn't sure if it was the light or if there really was a white filmy shape sitting on the ledge.

Phillip found Marilee sitting in the kitchen, drinking coffee, and staring into space. "Why are you up so early this morning?"

Marilee explained about her dream and then her trip to the attic. When she got to the part about the conversation, Phillip choked on his coffee.

"Do you mean you actually talked to the ghost?" he asked.

"I think I did, and I am positive Hannah almost revealed herself to me as I was leaving."

"I don't even have an answer to that," he replied.

They both sat quietly for a while sipping coffee, and then Marilee said, "I don't think we should mention this to anyone, not Jeannie nor the partners and especially not the kids when they come for Christmas."

"I agree. The less said about this to outsiders, the better. The kids would never come to visit if they knew you were conversing with ghosts, or they would be sending you to a special place."

Breakfasts continued but in a very quiet fashion as both Marilee and Phillip were thinking about what had happened and were trying to make sense of it.

The rest of the week ran smoothly at the winery and the B&B. There were several guests staying on the weekend, and a few people had heard about the winery and came to visit and taste the wine. The phone was ringing with compliments from some of the invited guests who had been at the grand opening.

Marilee decided she had some free time and would check out the files at the church again this week. She called Jeannie, but she was busy, so she called her friend at the church, and he was able to be there one afternoon later in the week. Marilee was relieved that Jeannie was unable to come as she knew it would be difficult not to tell her about her visit with Hannah.

Her visit to the church was a disappointment as nothing new about the Gillham family was discovered. It was now only ten days until Christmas, so Marilee packed up all her notes when she left the church and took them home and tucked them in the filing cabinet. This project would have to wait until next year.

Two days before Christmas, it snowed, and the area looked like a winter wonderland. There was snow sticking to the all the trees, making them look like they had been decorated by Jack Frost. It covered the long grass in the fields tidying up the messy fall look. Christmas lights that had been strung on bushes now peeked out from beneath a blanket of snow, giving them a diffused look. It really looked like an old-fashioned Christmas.

The family would be arriving on Christmas Eve, and Marilee couldn't wait to have her grandchildren in the house. She just hoped Hannah would behave, and she decided to put some soft music in the upstairs hall in case she started singing again like she did at Thanksgiving.

Everyone arrived the next day, and as usual, it was chaotic for a while as presents and suitcases were brought in from the cars. As well, the boys had to run through the house checking out all the spots they remembered. This year, they had Amanda following them everywhere as she could run and climb stairs now. It was definitely not a silent night on Christmas Eve.

The family were staying until the end of the week this year as no one had to travel to other places. This would mean there would be time for sledding and playing in the snow as well as touring the new winery.

After days outside in the snow and a lot of snacking, everyone slept soundly at night. There was no mention of sounds coming from the attic. Marilee did, however, make sure she said her prayer for peace each night just in case.

She was sad to see the grandchildren leave at the end of the week but was ready for some downtime. Now Marilee needed to clean her house and prepare some food to take to the New Year's Eve party at Jeannie and Ralph's house.

As Marilee and Phillip toasted peace in their house once more that evening at dinner, they reflected on all the things they had experienced this past year. Both agreed it had been a good year with just enough excitement to keep it interesting.

"If next year is as successful as this one, we are truly blessed," said Phillip. "Next year, our winery will be complete, including the crushing and vats, the bottling and storage part."

Marilee added, "By the end of next year, I hope to have all the families figured out and their destinations discovered. Maybe Hannah will know what happened to her family and to Peter. That way, she can either move on or be happy here."

"I'll drink to that."

JANUARY

The house was quiet; the Christmas decorations were all put away, and no guests were expected for months. Marilee and Phillip had their house back for a while. It was quite nice sitting by the fire with a hot cup of coffee having no immediate commitment. The Christmas holidays had been busy with the opening of the Barn, the family coming for Christmas, and other social events in the community.

"How would you like to go to California for a few weeks this month?" asked Phillip.

Marilee almost choked on her coffee. "Are you kidding? How long have you been thinking about this? Where would we stay? Could we get tickets this late?"

"I have tentatively booked tickets and have until tomorrow to firm up with the airline. There is a small winery that has a few cottages for rent, and we could start there for a few days. Then we could visit other wineries and find accommodation as we go. I don't think it is too busy at this time of year, so it shouldn't be a problem."

"Wow. You really have been planning this."

"I think it would be good to check out how some of the wineries in California run their businesses, especially when combined with a bed-and-breakfast or a hotel. It also would be nice to take a small holiday before the next season gets busy. Nothing is being started on the building until mid-February, so this may be our last chance to get away."

Marilee was already thinking about new decorating ideas and warmer temperatures. "I can be ready to go in two days."

Two days later, Marilee and Phillip flew into San Francisco and headed immediately to the Napa Valley. This, of course, was the most famous wine region in California, and Phillip particularly wanted to visit the legendary Robert Mondavi Winery which was celebrating a hundred years in the business.

They had not booked reservations, except for the first and last night of their trip, so the first stop was a travel bureau to obtain a list of B&Bs in the area. There were a lot of choices, but they really wanted to stay at ones connected to a winery. Within minutes, they had their next three nights booked at a picturesque B&B beside a winery in one of the many valleys.

The next three days were spent visiting the wineries, taking tours that they could have conducted, and on several occasions, having the chance to talk to an owner about the winery. Once an owner knew they were running a winery, the tours became more personal, and they saw parts of the operation not always open to the public.

"This is a great way to see the wine region of a foreign country," said Phillip. "We could do this in all the wine regions of the world."

"You are forgetting that we only speak English," answered Marilee.

They knew it would be impossible to see all the wineries in California and so decided to concentrate only on the area around San Francisco. This would give them some time to return to the city and explore a bit before they had to leave.

Their next stop was Sonoma County. This was where it all began when in the 1850s, a pioneer winemaker introduced European grapes to Sonoma, and the California wine industry was created. One of the highlights of the trip was to travel through the valley over the vineyards in a hot air balloon. Again, they found some delightful small inns as accommodation. Marilee picked up a few tips and ideas for Loyalist House, but as the background was more Spanish than British, she wasn't sure a lot of their menus would work. It certainly was fun, though, to be on the other side of the table so to speak and be waited on and served rather than serving.

Soon, though, it was time to leave San Francisco and fly to Phoenix where they would spend a week just relaxing before returning home. The resort they had booked was small and delightful with many things to do in the area, but Marilee and Phillip spent most of their time sitting by the pool and truly relaxing. Marilee did manage to fit in a few shopping excursions during that week, while Phillip read his new books about California wineries.

The trip home was noneventful, and both agreed they were ready to get back to the house. It had been a whirlwind tour, and they were already talking about doing the southern California wineries next winter.

*   *   *

Hannah realized after several days of flitting about the house, both the house she knew and the unfamiliar one, that she was really alone. The nice lady and the others she often saw doing strange things were not around. Some of the lights came on at various times and turned off by themselves, which was really puzzling. Why would they need lights on if they were not home? It did give her more freedom to wander into rooms she had not been in before. It seemed as though during the day she was visiting the unfamiliar house, but at night it became her own house again.

One evening as she stood staring to the west, the vision of her uncle William's farm appeared. Her mother and Aunt Elizabeth were sitting by the fire knitting as the children played on the floor. Uncle William was working at some papers at the table, and her brother was just staring at the window. Could he see her watching? Hannah wasn't sure.

Suddenly, there was the sound of steps on the wooden boards outside the front door of the small cabin. William jumped up and grabbed his rifle. The women gathered the children and took them behind the blanket into the bedroom. Andrew went to the other side of the room and picked up the other rifle. Their swift, automatic movement almost looked like a practiced routine.

"Who is it?" asked William in a loud voice.

"It is Peter Gillham, a neighbor of David and Sarah."

Sarah gasped and came into the main room of the cabin. "Ask him if he is alone?"

"Are you alone?"

"Yes, I am."

William opened the door, and Peter stepped inside. It was strange for Peter to see Mrs. Van Every again. He had not seen her since before Hannah had been killed, and he wasn't sure what to say.

Mrs. Van Every, however, was a kind woman and went to Peter and immediately hugged him. "Peter, it is lovely to see you again. Are you alone or have your parents returned with you? How did you find us?"

Peter then related his story about leaving his parents and returning to the farm. "I apologize for entering your home, and I stumbled across the loose bricks in the pantry and found the letters."

"Were there any letters from David in that spot?" Mrs. Van Every quickly asked.

"Yes, there was one dated September. He had returned to the house with his militia group on their way to St. Davids. He said he was fine and surviving, but food was in short supply, and the weather was starting to get colder. He said he took warmer clothes with him. I am sorry I read your letter, but I wanted to know where you had gone."

"Peter, you have given me good news about my husband. Thank you. What are you going to do now?"

"I want to stay here and run my father's farm, but I am now old enough to be in the militia and am afraid once someone tells about my family I will be considered a traitor. I need to go far enough away from the fighting to be safe. I am a good worker and could be a help on a farm."

William stepped forward and spoke. "We could certainly use another hand here, but we are too close to the fighting. We never know if either side will descend on the house and take over the land or worse. I have another brother who lives to the northwest closer to Newark. He has only young children, and a hardworking, strong young man would be a help to him. I do not think he could pay you, but he could certainly provide food and a place to sleep. I will write you a letter to take with you, but first, you must stay here tonight and leave in the morning. I am afraid you will have to sleep in the barn as our small cabin is full."

"I appreciate your kindness. Thank you."

Elizabeth had been working by the stove and brought over a plate of leftover food for Peter. "I wonder if you have eaten on your journey here. Eat this before you turn in tonight."

Peter realized he was starving as all the food he had packed for the journey was gone. As he ate, he told Mrs. Van Every and the others about how his mother did not like being on the other side of the river, and how starting over again had been very difficult for her. He realized after he had left the house and was settling in the barn for the night that no one had mentioned a word about Hannah. It was probably for the better as it would have made him very sad, and he figured it would do the same to Hannah's family.

Peter was sorry Hannah had been killed by the soldiers, and he felt he was to blame. He had loved her and wondered if the family knew they wanted to be married. He wondered what she had done with the letters he wrote. It made him sad to know that now he was truly alone and had lost the person he loved. He slept fitfully that night and was awake and packing up as Hannah's brother came into the barn.

"I should just take a gun and shoot you for causing my sister's death," said Andrew.

Peter noticed he was not carrying a gun, so he began to talk to him. "You cannot believe how terribly sorry I am that she was killed. I will tell you something even my parents do not know. Your sister and I were in love and planned to get married as soon as she was old enough. I have never lost anyone before, and this is a terrible feeling. Every night as I am trying to go to sleep, all the memories of the things we said to each other and the plans we had keep coming back into my head. I do not think I will ever forget her. I wish this war had never happened."

Peter had to stop talking as he had a lump in his throat that was about to choke him.

Andrew's mood changed suddenly after listening to Peter talk. He said, "I have not told anyone this as I know they would think I am crazy, and my mother would just be upset all over again. I think that Hannah is still living in the house but as a ghost. Please do not think I am crazy, and you must not tell anyone. Before we left, I think she was trying to stop us by doing strange things in the house and actually trying to bump into us. I do not know if that is even possible, but I just had this feeling that she was in the room. I still think sometimes even though we are here at my uncle's farm, she is still watching us from the house."

"I went to the house one night," said Peter. "I did not see anything odd, but I was worried I might meet a soldier hiding in the house. Maybe I was too focused on other things."

"I do not really know if there are ghosts or why they are there, and I cannot ask anyone here. I wish I could go with you to Uncle Samuel's farm, but I know Mother will never let me go away from here, and Uncle William does need me."

"You need to stay here with your family. If anything happened to you on the journey, it would break your mother's heart. She has lost enough already, and it must be difficult for her with your father away fighting and not knowing where or how he is."

"You are right of course, Peter, but I am old enough now to be fighting as well. If strangers come to the farm here, I am to say I am only fourteen so they will not take me into the militia. My mother worries about all of us. You know she now will be worrying about you as well."

"I suppose she will. I think my mother must be so upset with me for leaving. I did not leave a note when I left as I knew my father would come after me and drag me back. I left a note for them at the supply depot on the other side of the river where I crossed. I am sure at some point when he goes for supplies, they will give him the note."

The boys continued to talk for some time before William came to the barn with the letter for Peter. He said the family were waiting for him to come and say goodbye before he left, so they all returned to the cabin. There were tears and hugs and well wishes, and of course, a package of food for the journey.

"You must remember to stop here on your way back to the farm after this terrible war is over," said Elizabeth. "We will always be pleased to see you."

"And please do stop at the Van Every farm as well when you return, Peter," said Mrs. Van Every as she gave him another hug. She then whispered in his ear, "Hannah told me before she was killed you two wanted to be married, so I always will think of you as another son." She wiped the tears from her eyes as she stepped back from him.

Peter did not know what to say. The tears were welling up in his eyes, and he did not trust his voice to work properly. Instead, he took Mrs. Van Every's hands, squeezed them gently, and mouthed the words "thank you."

Peter took a deep breath, smiled at everyone, gave a small salute to Andrew, turned, and began the journey that would change the direction his life would take.

Hannah had been watching all this and was sobbing as she saw Peter walk away from the farm. She could not always hear conversation but could always see what was happening. She saw Peter begin walking away from everyone in the opposite direction from the river and knew he was leaving the area.

She was furious that she didn't know where he was going. She began to fly about the house knocking over things as she went.

The lamps in the living room were on the floor, cushions from the couch were scattered around, and most of the pictures on the wall hung at precarious angles. Next, she went to the dining room and smashed a few dishes before going toward the kitchen.

In the pantry, Hannah found a five-pound bag of sugar and took it into the kitchen and poured it on the floor before flying up the dumbwaiter to the bedroom area. In each room, she pulled the blankets and spreads from the beds and tossed pillows on the floor. Next, she went to the attic and opened the trunk. The clothes inside were dumped out, and she then proceeded to rip the head off her doll, removed all the letters, and tossed them beside the clothes.

As she flew about the room, the breeze scattered the paper across the floor, making it look like a windstorm had been inside the attic.

She was becoming a bit tired by now, so she sat by the window and sobbed. Hannah sobbed and sobbed. She knew Peter had gone away and would never return. She suspected her brother had something to do with it. What had he and Peter been talking about in the barn at Uncle William's farm? Why had her mother given him such a big hug as he was leaving? How would she ever find out what was going on with no one in the house anymore? Hannah decided the only thing she could do was to cry and cry until someone showed up at the house.

It was winter now, cold and windy. There was some snow on the ground but fortunately not too much to make walking in the woods difficult. Peter had found some old papers and feed sacks in the barn and used them as insulation in his shoes and his coats. He was wearing two pairs of pants and all the shirts he brought with him. Wearing so much clothing made his coat tight, so the wind seemed to go right through the fabric. He tried to keep in the woods to avoid meeting any soldiers, but he worried he might come across First Nations hunting parties that were known to be in the area. He wasn't sure whether he feared them or the wild animals more. He had seen some small rabbit tracks in the snow but no footprints. William had given him the directions to follow, and so far, he felt he was on the right trail. It would probably take him three days, which meant spending two nights in the woods unless he found a farm and could sleep in a barn.

Darkness came early the first night, and it was cloudy, so Peter had to stop before he really wanted to. He found a spot in the trees that was protected by some rocks and had small bushes around it. He had been gathering evergreen branches as he walked so he would have some to make a lean to for the night. He made his humble sleeping place and sat under the protection. He had eaten some of the food he carried the last hour he walked. Peter knew the smell of food might attract animals, and he did not want visitors in the night.

As he sat alone and cold, he thought back to his life on the farm by the river. The work had been hard, but up until the last few months, he felt safe and was happy being with his family.

Peter remembered the first time he saw Hannah. She was so nicely dressed, and her long curly hair hung down her back below the edge of her bonnet. She kept looking over to where he was talking with the other boys. She had been watching him. The only time he could really talk to her was when the two families were together usually at the dinner table at one of the farms.

There had been a few times as well when the parents were busy talking, and all the children had gone outside to play. Hannah's brother, Andrew, always seemed to be there and was very protective of his two sisters. Peter's thoughts then turned to Andrew's comment about Hannah's spirit still being in the house. Peter did not know much about ghosts and did not understand how or why she was still there, and it bothered him to think of her alone and possibly waiting for him.

His thoughts seemed to drift from Hannah alone in the house, to the night she was killed. He could see vividly the gunfire at the shore and later her parents by the river. The same scene played over and over in his head with no conclusion.

Suddenly, a strange noise interrupted his thoughts. Peter opened his eyes and saw a racoon just about to stick his nose into the pack where the food was. He realized it was almost daylight and could see the racoon clearly. He slowly reached beside him and grabbed his gun, stood up, and packed the gunpowder down the barrel. The racoon was quite brazen and did not even move at all while keeping his eyes on Peter, and one paw on the pack. Peter aimed, pulled the trigger, and shot at the critter.

He was a good marksman, and in an instant, the coon lay on the ground beside the food pack. Peter thought the skin would make a great hat but did not want to take the time to skin the animal now.

The sun was beginning to light up the eastern sky, so Peter decided to begin the second day of his journey.

As he was walking and munching on some bread and cheese, he remembered the dream he had in the night. It was frustrating as it had gone round in circles. Maybe tonight would be the next chapter, he thought to himself.

Today turned out to be sunny, and although it was still cold, the sun seemed warm and made the landscape look more welcoming. Again, Peter stuck to the bush to avoid being seen. He had walked for several hours when he noticed smoke on the horizon. He stopped to see if there was a way to get past the smoke without being seen. He would have to go a considerable distance out of his way to avoid it. He decided to turn to the north and stay along the edge of the bush, and later he could turn back to the west.

He had walked another hour and was just stopping to get a drink when he heard a noise behind him. It sounded like a horse. Peter turned, and to his horror, he saw five horses following him. It looked like a First Nations hunting party. How long had they been there? He stopped, put his gun barrel to the ground, and waited.

The small hunting party allowed their horses to walk slowly toward Peter. When they were about three feet from him, the rider in the center dismounted and walked toward Peter. He did not take his gun or grab Peter. Instead, in halting English, he asked him who he was and where he was going.

Peter gave his name as Peter Van Every and told him he was on the way to see Samuel Van Every, his uncle.

The Indian nodded his head and said, "Father David Van Every?"

Peter decided instantly the answer had to be, "Yes."

"You are also friend. Come with us."

Peter knew he had no choice and wasn't sure what would happen next, but he took one of the riders hands and was pulled up in front of him onto the horse.

It was nice to have a ride and give his legs a rest, but it was quite nerve-wracking not knowing what they would do to him or where they were taking him. He hoped the word friend was a good omen.

Peter was not used to riding a horse, let alone for another hour. It was tiring sitting straight and not leaning back as the rider behind him was quite close. When one of the other riders had taken his gun and pack, Peter was quite nervous and somewhat reluctant to give it up. Now he felt a bit relieved as it took both hands to hang on to the horse's main and stay centered.

The smoke he had seen earlier was now visible as was the First Nations hunting camp. There were about ten tepees and what seemed like an army of First Nations watching as the hunting party and extra rider returned to camp. They rode right to the fire, and all dismounted and indicated that Peter should as well.

Peter stood beside the horse and wasn't sure his legs would carry him if he had to walk somewhere. His stomach was in a knot and doing somersaults all at the same time. He was sure he was going to vomit. The rider who had spoken to him earlier went into one of the tents, and talking could be heard, but the language was foreign.

The flap on the tepee opened, and a tall man, obviously the chief, stepped out. He must have been the most important member of this small band as everyone stopped what they were doing and watched him. He then approached Peter, asking his name.

Peter decided to stay with the Van Every name as it seemed to have worked so far. The chief then told him how his grandfather had been their friend in the past and he would also be their friend. Peter was invited into the tepee along with four others. Only the chief spoke English but translated everything so Peter could understand.

The warmth from bodies and a small fire inside the tepee made Peter drowsy, but he fought to stay awake. He didn't really understand all the statements they were making but heard them say tomorrow two of their members would ride with him to his uncle's farm. He was then invited to eat dinner with the chief.

After dinner, Peter was taken to another tepee where there was straw on the ground for a bed. His gun and his pack were already in the tent. He decided his fate was in their hands and whatever happened was meant to be, so he said a prayer and lay down and immediately fell asleep.

Noises outside awakened him, but it was still dark. He got up anyway, gathered his things, and opened the flap. The two guides were there with three horses waiting for him. They helped him stow his gun and pack, and he somehow managed to get on the horse by himself.

Thus began the last part of his journey. Peter worried the whole time about how he could tell Samuel he was Peter Van Every and have him believe it. He did not know whether or not these two spoke English as they had not said a word to him or to each other.

Shortly after midday, they reached a small knoll that overlooked a farm in the valley. According to the directions William had given him, this should be Samuel's farm. The two guides dismounted and took the reins of the horse Peter was riding. They handed him his gun and pack and gestured for him to go toward the house. Peter bowed slightly, thanked them, and walked down the hill. He turned around once, and saw they were waiting until he was at the house. When he was at the door, he turned to look once more, but they had disappeared. It would be easier to tell Samuel who he really was without fear of being discovered as a fraud.

He knocked at the door and called out his name. It was still a few minutes before the door opened, and he heard some scrambling and chairs moving inside. A tall man who looked almost identical to William opened the door. He had a gun in his hand. He looked Peter up and down, and in a loud, strong voice, he asked, "Who are you, and what do you want?"

"Sir, I am Peter Gillham. My family were neighbors of your brother David. No one can live along the river now, so your brother William suggested I come to see if you needed a farmhand. I have a letter from him."

"Come inside," said Samuel.

Peter handed Samuel the letter and waited. He could hear children's voices behind a wall and someone shushing them.

Finally, Samuel said, "You can bring the children out, Hannah. It is safe."

When Peter heard the name Hannah, his heart skipped a beat. But Hannah this time was Samuel's wife and much older than his Hannah. It was sad, though, as it reminded him he would have to break the news to them of his Hannah's death.

The remainder of the day was spent telling the family all the details of their relatives and the events of the war that had occurred. They did know war had been declared but had no idea what had happened in the past eight months. Peter also told them, somewhat sheepishly, how he had led the First Nations to believe he was a Van Every and about the reception he had received.

Samuel, after a bit of thinking, said, "I think it would be in your best interest and ours if you continued to think of yourself as Peter Van Every. No one needs to know the truth about your parents. Being our son who has returned from helping my brother will work just fine. People do not ask others their business right now, and besides, our nearest neighbors are a long ways away. You must call us Mother and Father, so the story is believable. Hannah, we have a new son to add to our family. We are now five."

*   *   *

FEBRUARY

Marilee and Phillip had paid the taxi driver and unlocked the back door to enter the house. To their horror, the kitchen was a mess.

"Just leave everything here, and we will see what else is disturbed," said Phillip. "Don't touch anything until after the police have been here."

Marilee was horrified to see her house in such a state. "Who did this, and why?"

"That's what we hope to find out."

As they walked from room to room, the mess continued, although it seemed to be mostly furniture turned upside down and things knocked over. There were a few broken items, but it was as though someone had done this while walking on a path through the house. The upstairs had a similar pattern of destruction as did the attic.

Marilee was becoming a bit suspicious as to who the culprit was but didn't say anything yet. When she returned to the kitchen and walked into the pantry, she saw a bag of sugar had been dumped on the floor but not in a normal way. The sugar formed a perfect pyramid shape on the floor. Sugar would not normally fall this way on the floor. Marilee wanted to touch it but was afraid it would ruin the shape if she did.

"Phillip, you need to see this in the pantry."

"How did that happen?" Phillip asked as he saw the odd structure. "Is it glued like that, or what?"

"Don't touch it. I think all this might be the work of Hannah. She may have been very angry about something and did this to get someone's attention. She may have seen Peter."

"Do we call the police or what?" asked Phillip angrily.

"Maybe we should call Detective Barrens as he knows about our ghost before we tell anyone else."

"Good idea," said Phillip as headed to the phone.

The call to Detective Barrens was timely as he was on duty and able to come to their home within the hour. He knew the background of the ghost but was still astounded at what he found and what he did not find.

There were no finger prints on any item either smashed or overturned. The sugar incident had him totally perplexed. As he did not really believe in ghosts, he was reluctant to blame it on Hannah but could not come up with another answer. He did feel calling in the police to investigate might not be a wise thing as they would not find anything different, and word of these things always seemed to get into the press.

"I will personally look into reports of any incidents in the area to see if there were other break-ins and get back to you. Take some pictures and then you can begin to put things back to normal. I really want to see what happens when you touch that sugar."

"Let's start with that one," said Marilee as she pulled her camera from her suitcase.

As soon as the photo was taken, Marilee touched the perfect pile of sugar, and it immediately collapsed as sugar naturally would.

The room was silent. Even Marilee was thinking maybe she wanted to go to a hotel tonight rather than stay in the house.

"Wow," said Phillip and the detective at the same time.

Detective Barrens left rather quickly after the picture of the sugar was taken and said he would be in touch with them within the next few days.

It was early afternoon, so Phillip and Marilee changed into some work clothes and began to return their house to some order. They took lots of pictures in each room, and by dinner, the two lower floors were back in order. The attic cleanup was next, but neither wanted to go up to tackle it.

"Let's leave the attic until tomorrow," said Phillip, hoping Marilee would agree.

"I think that's a good idea. I can't really do any more today."

"I am going to order some dinner to be delivered tonight. Does pizza sound good?"

"Wonderful."

Phillip ordered the pizza, opened a bottle of wine, and the two weary travellers spent the evening talking about all the possibilities of how this weird event happened in their house.

When it came time for bed, they both procrastinated, unpacking clothes and putting them away. Marilee had to find a glass for some water, and Phillip had to look for a new toothbrush. Eventually, they were in bed but reluctant to turn out the light.

"This is ridiculous," said Marilee. "We have slept here every other night knowing that Hannah was in the attic and not always knowing what she would do."

Phillip added, "I know. I never really thought about her before, but tonight, I am a bit worried."

"I think I may read a bit, even though I am exhausted," said Marilee. "Why don't you try that new book you picked up in California?"

"Good idea."

They both read for a while and eventually turned off the lights and went to sleep. Marilee awoke with a start. She sat up, noticed the room was semi light, and looked at the clock.

"Good grief, Phillip. It is nine thirty. We have slept in. I guess we were tired, and with the time change, we managed to sleep the whole night, and I don't think anything happened."

They both put on their housecoats and went down to the kitchen, not knowing what they would find. Everything looked normal; nothing was out of place, spilled, or turned upside down.

"Maybe this was a one-time event because something happened to upset Hannah," said Marilee. Maybe I need to go up to the attic one day and see if she can still hear me. Maybe she will actually talk to me."

"That's a lot of maybes," said Phillip.

"I must find out where Peter went by the end of this month," she added. "That information will help answer many questions."

Today, Phillip hoped he would get an answer from Detective Barrens that might be more concrete than Marilee's ghost activities. "I am going into town to the police station and then find Dave and Mike to see when they are starting the new building. I probably won't be back until late afternoon."

"That's fine," Marilee answered. "I have lots to do here today."

Marilee decided she had to tell Jeannie about the house and ask her if she had found out any more information about Peter. She called Jeannie, and within ten minutes, she came over to see the pictures.

Jeannie confirmed they had seen no one in the driveway the whole time Marilee and Phillip were away. She and Ralph had driven in the driveway several times on purpose after it snowed to make it look like someone was home.

"I can't believe that sugar pyramid," said Jeannie. "Was the sugar hard or soft when you touched it?"

Marilee retold the whole story and then asked her about the research to change the topic. She still did not want to tell anyone about her interaction with Hannah that day in the attic.

"I have found a farm belonging to a Samuel Van Every that was sold during the war. It was near Newark, and the land had been granted to Samuel Van Every for his service to the crown during the American Revolution. There really was no mention of a Peter Gillham anywhere," said Jeannie. "Our friend at the church said he had no other information that would be relevant. Do you think he changed his name because of his parents? Did they do that kind of thing back then?"

"I have no idea," said Marilee.

Marilee was beginning to think the only way to solve this mystery was for Hannah to be able to communicate with her. But would that even be possible? She now thought she might have to begin researching talking to spirits. One thing just seemed to lead to another and further investigation.

"Did you research any further than Samuel selling his farm?" she asked Jeannie.

"No. Only that far."

"What if we went to the next generation to see what they did and if he kept the Van Every name?" Marilee asked.

"Well, it probably can't hurt."

"Let's go back to the church and see if we can find out more about the next generation," Marilee suggested. "How about tomorrow afternoon?"

"OK by me," said Jeannie.

It was settled they would call the church to see if John would be able to help them tomorrow, and if so, they would meet there after lunch.

Life at Loyalist House returned to normal over the next few days. It was quiet as no guests were expected until Valentine's Day. Marilee had managed to even return the attic to a normal state. She had carried on a gentle conversation with Hannah but had no response of any kind. If Hannah was in the attic, she was not revealing herself.

Phillip, Mike, and Dave were very involved with the start of the new production building for the winery. The building permits were all in place, and the construction crew were hired. They just had to take care of the day-to-day supervision. Everything was going according to plan, and with no hick-ups, the place would be ready by late August just in time for harvest.

Phillip had contacted Detective Barrens about related break-ins, but there had been none in the area, so even though he was reluctant to do so, Phillip agreed that it might have been Hannah who had caused the mess in the house.

The weather was even cooperating. There was a bit of snow on the ground, but the temperatures were hovering around the freezing mark which made it ideal not only for construction but also for pruning the grape vines. Phillip was afraid to mention out loud how well things were going for fear of jinxing something, so he just kept the thoughts to himself.

Marilee and Jeannie had quite a successful afternoon at the church looking for information on the extended Van Every family. John had found some other files for them to look at, and as Marilee was on the last page of the third file, she whistled, "It says here that after the war, the Van Every farm on the river was sold to a neighbor. It doesn't list another property as being purchased though."

Jeannie was rereading the file she looked at the other day just to see if she had missed anything. "There is nothing about a Peter Van Every owning a property near Newark. This just talks about a Samuel Van Every owning it but doesn't say anything else."

John walked into the small room at that point and announced, "We are closing for today in ten minutes. Will you be returning soon? Is there any other direction you might like to take in your search?"

Marilee quickly asked, "Do you have any marriage or birth certificates around that might help us connect the families?"

"We do have a limited number because as I mentioned earlier, many were destroyed when the town was burned. I shall see what I can find for you. When do you think you will come again?"

Jeannie and Marilee looked at each other, and both were thinking tomorrow, but to be fair to John, Marilee said, "Maybe early next week if that would work for you."

"I shall have the files for you by Tuesday," John replied.

"That will be great, and we do so appreciate your help," added Jeannie.

When John had left the room, Marilee said quietly to Jeannie, "We are either going to have to take him out for dinner to repay his kindness or give a sizable donation to this church."

"I agree," replied Jeannie.

That night after dinner, Marilee wondered what had happened while she was away. She may have missed a few dreams that would give some clues to the mess as well as some more information about Peter. This was like missing several important episodes of a TV drama and then trying to catch up on who was doing what. She actually hoped she might have a dream tonight to fill in the missing parts. But it was not to be. There was no sobbing in the attic, and Marilee slept soundly through the entire night.

The next morning, she complained to Phillip, "You know when I want to sleep through the night, I usually don't, and this time, I wanted to be disturbed, and guess what, I slept."

"I can't believe you are hoping to be disturbed and not wanting to sleep, and I don't think you can make a ghost do anything."

"Well, I do have to find out what's going on, or this could all happen again when we have our next guests."

"True," said Phillip as he read the paper and sipped his coffee.

Valentine's Day arrived, and the guests checked into Loyalist House. They were polite and quiet and spent most of the weekend attending the ice wine festival and visiting wineries. Phillip was pleased they had visited the winery and were very impressed with several of Loyalist House wines.

The best part of the weekend, though, was the quietness in the attic. There was no sobbing or crashing of furniture or any evidence of spirit life in the house. Even Marilee was relieved.

MARCH

Hannah's favorite place to be was at the window of the attic where she watched to see if there was any sign of Peter returning. She was also watching for soldiers in case one might be her father. There were a few soldiers on the river but mostly British who were travelling down the river toward Newark.

One day, she saw a boat travelling down the river, but it slowed and landed at the dock. Hannah sat up and began to watch intently. Two soldiers got out of the boat, and then it pushed off and continued down the river. As the soldiers climbed the hill, she realized it was her father and another soldier. Hannah flew down to the kitchen just in time to see them walk in the back door.

David Van Every put his pack on the floor and suggested to his friend he do the same for now. "It looks like we will have to do a bit of cleaning up as the guests who were here did not see the need to be tidy."

"At least, we will have a comfy place to sleep and a real roof over our head for a bit," said the friend.

They began the task of picking up broken crockery and upended furniture. David remarked, "Sarah would not think this is neat enough, but it will do for us."

"Will we have the necessary seeds to plant a crop this season?"

"I hope so," answered David. "I had some seed stored in the barn, so I may have to check to see if anyone is still here or at the next farm. We have about a month here before we will have to sign up again as long as no major fighting erupts in this area. I appreciate you coming to help me plant my crops, but I am sorry about your parents' death. You may stay here on this farm as long as I am here. I hope soon my family can return home as well. God willing."

The two men scrounged around the kitchen for food but found nothing as everything edible had been either taken by looters or eaten by mice. "Let us go to the Gillham farm before dark to see if Eli is still there. Maybe he has a bit of food to spare," said David.

Hannah was quite excited after hearing the conversation. It sounded like her father had returned at least for a while. She decided to watch them as they walked to the Gillham farm. Maybe the same thing would happen if she concentrated, and she could hear what was going on. She heard them talking as they walked even after they were out of site. Her father seemed to be explaining how the farms used to be, who the Gillhams were, and why they had left. When they reached the small cabin, David knocked on the door and identified himself so as not to frighten Eli and his family. He assumed the family would still be here.

"Good evening, Mr. Van Every. Come in. We are very surprised to see you," said Eli. "Is the war over?"

"No, Eli, I am afraid it is not. Our enlistment ended, and as the fighting is out on the lake, we are not needed now. This is a fellow militia man and friend George. He has lost his family and has come home with me to help plant the crops for this season. I came to ask if there was any seed to plant this spring, or has it been stolen as well?"

"When the soldiers started coming and looting farms, I took the seed from both barns and hid it in a small shed under the floor. I hope it has not sprouted or rotted. There is enough to plant about ten acres of wheat and barley."

"You are a clever man, Eli. Mr. Gillham should be proud to have you as his friend and manager. Is there any news of the Gillham family?"

Hannah had been listening carefully, and at this point, she became very excited and really concentrated so she would hear the answer.

Eli began, "Young Mr. Peter came back to the farm as he was not happy living over the river. He said his mother was also very unhappy, but his father remained true to his word and is staying with the Americans. I told him no one was here, and it was not safe, so he went to your brother William's farm to see your wife. The fighting was very close to here, so he did not stay. We have had soldiers come here several times, but they see I am old and black, so they think I am useless. They leave us alone.

"You are a very wise man, Eli. I think this spring we should plant the crops together and share the harvest. If we put it in the fields between the houses away from the river, we might manage to have some food for next winter."

"I will be ready to help you," replied Eli.

At that point, Sarah came from behind the curtain with two plates of food for David and George. The men thanked her and hungrily ate the delicious meal and continued their conversation about farming practises.

Hannah was thrilled that her father would be in the house for a while. She might be able to hear and see things to help her understand how long this war would continue. She floated back up to the attic, found her doll in pieces, and decided to sew the head back on. She noticed that the mess she had created in the attic was gone. This must mean the nice lady downstairs had returned. She was happy about that but still sad about her beloved Peter not being there.

After the doll was repaired, Hannah sat by the window and sobbed. But tonight, the sobs were very quiet, and every once in a while, a small humming tune could be heard in between a sob.

* * *

Marilee awoke in the morning and realized she had dreamt about Hannah. She had been worried that she had no dreams about the house since she had returned from California. Now she was sure Hannah was still in the attic. It was a dilemma whether to go to the attic and try to make contact with Hannah or to wait for dreams to give her more information. She decided to think about it for a bit before doing anything. Today, she was meeting Jeannie at the church to check out birth and marriage certificates to see what they could find. Maybe today would be a lucky day.

At breakfast, Phillip was very excited as the roof trusses were arriving for the building. By the end of the month, the walls would be up, and the inside would begin to take shape. The building inspectors were scheduled to come after the roof was on, but hopefully, everything would be fine.

Dave had heard a rumor that someone had expressed a concern that such a large structure was being built so near to residential houses. The site had been approved for this zoning, so they weren't too worried, but one never knew.

Marilee and Jeannie met at the church, and before they went in to meet John, Marilee told Jeannie about her dream. She wondered why soldiers would be able to leave the militia and go to their homes for periods of time during a war.

"Let's ask John. He seems to know so much about life in this town during the war," Jeannie suggested.

"Good idea. Here he comes now."

Marilee asked John the question, and he told them that during the war, many of the locals who were basically conscripted by the British militia only signed up for a specific time period. When it ended, they were asked to reenlist; or if they were not needed because of location, the farmers in particular were given the opportunity to go home and take care of their farms.

"During the early part of 1813, most of the fighting was concentrated at the western end of Lake Erie and involved the naval divisions. Many of the local farmers did return and were home long enough to plant their crops. While they were away, it was a great hardship for their wives and families to try and keep the farm running." John continued as they walked to the file room in the basement, "Often, the wives would follow the troops to battle and could be seen searching on the battlefield after the fighting stopped to try and find loved ones who had been injured or killed. It really was a difficult time."

As they reached the workroom, Marilee and Jeannie saw John had put two more stacks of files on the front of the table. This man was amazing.

John said, "So today, we are looking at birth and marriage certificates. These are all the files we have starting at 1814 until 1820. Of course, this only applies to this area. I hope these will be of some help to you." He hesitated for a moment and then said, "I never asked you why you needed this information and why you have focused on the Van Every family? I know for sure some Van Every children were baptized here at the church, but they are all buried in a family plot at the Christian Warner Burial Ground. Have you visited there?"

"Yes, I have," answered Marilee. "That was the first place I found so many Van Everys. When I received the family genealogy from one of the relatives, it was easy to match up the names as they had done a thorough search. The one name we did not see was Hannah's. Would she be buried there in an unmarked grave or in another family grave with no record?"

"That could be the case. I know the cemetery spans the time period 1754 to 1833, so she should be buried there. Although there could be many possibilities why her name is not listed. She was a female minor, and as you think her death was just as the war was beginning, it might have been a hasty burial either there or another place."

"John, I am so glad we met you. The information you know and your knowledge of the files here is just invaluable," Jeannie responded.

"Well, thank you," said John humbly. "I really do enjoy learning about everyone's family. I have some other filing to do today, so I will leave you to your task. Come and find me if you need anything else."

Marilee and Jeannie settled into their pattern of silence as they looked for names that might help them connect Peter to any more of the Van Every family. Of course, they were not sure if he used the name Van Every or Gillham.

"Oh my," Jeannie almost shouted. "Here is the record of the marriage of Peter Van Every and Agnes Barry in 1816. It says Peter is the son of Samuel Van Every but was married in York."

Marilee jumped up and quickly moved over to Jeannie's table. "Let's look at that."

They read carefully three or four times but really only discovered the names, the dates, and the place. None of it really added up, especially the fact that he was married in York not Niagara. As usual, finding out one piece of information always led to researching another name or place.

"I must go back and reread the family history again. Maybe it will tell me how Peter got to York and who this Agnes Barry is. I confess I only skimmed the later parts thinking we would not need to know this," said Marilee.

Both Marilee and Jeannie went back to their files to see what else they could find. At the end of the day, they knew that Samuel sold the family farm in Niagara after the war and moved to the western end of Lake Ontario, once again becoming a pioneer and starting over to build a home and farm. On the ride home later, they both kept asking each other questions, but neither knew the answers.

They arrived at Loyalist House, and Jeannie commented, "I am coming in with you while you check the family tree to see what there is about Agnes Barry."

"Good idea," answered Marilee.

They walked in through the kitchen and straight on to Marilee's office. They did say hi to Phillip but kept on going. He knew better than to ask what they were up to.

"I am so stupid," said Marilee after she had scanned the back of the book. "If only I had read a bit further or looked at the back, I could have saved us an immense amount of work and a lot of frustration. I would never make a good detective."

"You have a lot of distractions with all that's going on in your life right now," said Jeannie, trying to console her. "At least we found out."

"I will reread this tonight to try and straighten out all this information in my mind," she said as she shut the book. "Once we get it all organized, you and I can decide where to go next with this. I have some interesting things to tell you, but I want to read this first."

Jeannie hated suspense, but she knew Marilee would not change her mind, so she just said, "Great, I'll see you tomorrow."

After dinner, Marilee read the genealogy of the family and eventually took it up to bed with her. When Phillip came to bed, she was fast asleep with the book on top of her still open.

*   *   *

Hannah was happier these days as her father was living in the house. The only problem was that he was rarely around during the day, and at night, he slept. He and George had been working hard to get ready to plant the crops, hopefully in the next few weeks. Today, she decided to try and look beyond the Van Every farm and see if she could see Peter. She knew he wasn't at Uncle William's anymore and didn't understand why he left and walked away from the river. She suddenly recalled her parents talking about another uncle who lived further away. Maybe he had gone there, but what was his name?

Hannah now knew if she thought of someone hard enough she could usually channel into their thoughts and often see her family. It had not worked for Peter, but he was not family. She decided to think about her mother while looking to the west. It worked. She could see her mother and aunt working together in the kitchen. Today was a bonus because she could hear what they were saying.

"I hope Peter made it safely to Samuel's farm," said Sarah. "I guess we will just have to trust he made it safely as there is no way of finding out."

"Have faith, Sarah," said Elizabeth. "What is meant to be will be."

"He is a good boy and would have made a wonderful husband for Hannah. They did not know David and I were aware of their secret courting. We felt it was harmless as they would just send notes to each other and talk when the occasion made it possible. We did not know they were meeting secretly at the river. We never would have allowed that in good times, let alone with a war pending. I sometimes feel it was my fault for being so preoccupied with everything else that was happening."

"You cannot blame yourself, Sarah. You know that none of us are in control of our own destiny. The Bible says our days are numbered from the beginning, and only God knows the plan."

"Yes. I do know that, but I am still sad."

Hannah had tears in her eyes as she hated to see her mother unhappy. She was sobbing once again while standing at the dining room window. However, she heard where Peter had gone. If she thought hard about her uncle Samuel, maybe she would be able to see him. The problem was she could not remember what he looked like as it had been a long time since they visited. Every time she tried to see his face in her mind, the only image that appeared was that of her father. Maybe they looked alike, and it was really him. Hannah tried again, but as always, it was her father's face she saw, and it was their house in the background.

She flew back up to the attic window and sobbed as she watched the river.

*   *   *

Marilee woke with a start. She had heard the sobbing in the night and had been a part of Hannah's dream. She was thrilled as this had not happened for a while. She now knew that Peter was at the farm of Samuel Van Every. She could hardly wait to tell Jeannie. Instead, she got up and started breakfast. Jeannie was coming over later, so she would tell her then. Marilee had decided to tell Jeannie about the incident in the attic when she was aware of Hannah's presence. She was unsure of whether to try to talk to Hannah again and felt Jeannie's input might help her decide.

Phillip came down for breakfast texting someone on his phone and looking like a thunder cloud.

"What's up in the world of wine?"

"I just had a text from Mike, and we are once again waiting for the approvals. Apparently, the electrical inspector will not approve all the work that's been completed. We were a bit worried when he showed up to do the inspection. He is a qualified inspector, but he's also related to the owner at Fox Hollow. I think his wife is the owner's sister. Now we have to redo some of the simple things like move outlets down an inch. We thought they were within the range, but the inspector is always right. This should be interesting."

"Can't you request a different inspector?"

"No. The town doesn't like that approach. As it is, the inspector can't come to reinspect until early April. It just all sounds a bit fishy to us."

"How far does that put you behind?"

"Well, about a month, unless we can speed up some of the later work. I just don't want to lose the trades we have lined up to do some of the interior work. The spots he has not approved are located at various places around the building, so you can't even finish a section anywhere. It's very frustrating."

"I don't understand why Fox Hollow is so opposed to this winery. You have been fighting them every step of the way."

"We think they had eyes on this property as it borders one side of theirs. He may have hoped to increase his acreage as he is a bit short of the required amount to be an estate winery because of the bush in the center. If someone called them on it, they could lose their status as an estate winery."

"I hope there are good fences at the back of the property."

"Hmm," said Phillip as he finished his coffee and walked out to the construction site.

Marilee tidied up the kitchen and was just starting the dishwasher when Jeannie knocked on the door.

"I know I'm early, but I woke up at five this morning thinking about all of this."

"I must have been channeling you as that's when I woke up and was thinking of phoning you. I had another dream last night."

Marilee proceeded to tell Jeannie about the dream and her visit with Hannah earlier. This was one of the few times Marilee had seen Jeannie speechless for several minutes.

Finally, Jeannie spoke, "What are you going to do now? Will you tell Hannah where Peter is?"

"No. I want to find out more about Peter and what he may be doing and how he met Agnes Barry before I tell her anything. I don't want her to become angry."

"Good idea. I was thinking maybe we should go on the Internet and look up some names in a Web site dedicated to finding ancestors."

"That might be a good idea. Let's try that on my computer before we go to the church today."

The two friends went off to Marilee's office and began searching for names. Both names appeared, but in order to find out more, they had to join the site and pay the entrance fee.

"What choice do we have now? They have us hooked," said Marilee.

Marilee joined the site, paid her money, and logged in. They found the name Agnes Barry quite easily but were mystified by her location. They assumed she would be from Niagara area, but instead she was from York on the other side of the lake. Agnes's father was a storekeeper in York and the town clerk. She and Peter Van Every were married in 1816. It also listed the newlyweds as moving to a one-hundred-acre farm bordered by Lake Ontario in Etobicoke Township.

"Agnes Barry must belong to a wealthy family," said Marilee. "We know Peter had no money at this time. It is too short a time to have sold his father's farm."

"Look at this map," Jeannie pointed out. "The location of this farm in Etobicoke is prime property today, and I think that is where there was a hospital on Queen Street. It's right on Queen

Street and is being made into condos now. Also, it goes north almost to Bloor Street. If this is true, he was quite a lucky young man and certainly married well."

"This is good information. Why didn't we try this site before? Let's look up Peter and see what we find."

They were hoping to find out if Peter Gillham and Peter Van Every were one and the same, but it only listed Peter Van Every from the time he came to York and was married. There was nothing prior to 1814. It did, however, list the eight children born to Peter and Agnes from 1817 to 1836.

"Look at the name of the second daughter," Jeannie exclaimed. "It's Hannah!"

"I know. Hannah was also Samuel's wife, but this is maybe a clue for us. Let's try Peter Gillham."

Peter Gillham was not listed, and neither were his parents. It was as if they had never existed. The property Mr. Gillham had owned on the river was listed as belonging to someone else.

"Let's try Samuel Van Every to see how many children he has," said Marilee as she typed in the names. "Here, it says he had five children—Peter, William, Mary, Elizabeth, and John. It says Peter's birth date is 1794. That would be logical. With the fire destroying many records in Newark during the war, it would be easy to change the facts. We may just have to accept that both Peters are the same."

"Unless you have some more dreams, Marilee."

APRIL

The snow was gone; the grass was starting to turn green, and some of the buds on the fruit trees looked ready to pop. Marilee's garden was overflowing with crocus daffodils and tulips. Spring was finally here. This was always such a welcome site after so many months of dirty snow and brown twigs. Along the river, forsythia bushes spilled their yellow blooms at every property line and fence row.

Of course with spring came the start of another tourist season. Marilee was in the process of spring cleaning the rooms before the first guests arrived midmonth. She loved to have the fabrics freshly washed and ironed, giving each room an almost new look. Of course, there was always something new and different from last year in each room.

This year, she found perfect leather-bound writing paper holders for each room while she was in California. She also removed one item from each room when a new one was added. This process kept the rooms from becoming too crowded and junky looking. It took her the better part of two weeks to accomplish the cleaning task, but once it was done, she could begin to spend some time on the Peter and Hannah story.

There had been no dreams at night now for about two weeks. Ever since she and Jeannie found out Peter had married at the end of the war, it was silent in the attic. The sobbing had stopped. Nothing was moved across the room.

One day, talking to Jeannie on the phone, Marilee said, "I haven't heard from Hannah at all lately. I am very tired at night from getting the rooms ready for the season, but I am also worried she heard us discovering that Peter married someone else. Maybe she left."

"Oh, I think if she heard our conversation, she would be furious. She does seem to have a temper when things don't go her way."

"True enough. I guess we will have to wait to find out what she's up to."

It didn't take long. That very night, Marilee had another dream.

*   *   *

Peter was enjoying staying with Samuel and Hannah Van Every. They really did treat him like a son. The two other children, William and Mary, were fun to be with as well. They were about five and six years younger than Peter, and they thought he was the best brother in the world because he gave them piggy back rides and played catch when he wasn't working.

Peter had been given the loft in the cabin as a place to sleep. It was always warm, and the sounds of the household and talking made him feel at home. He still felt the loneliness of being away from his real family and the sadness of Hannah's death in the darkness of the night. As much as he was loved by this family, he was not sure he could stay here forever.

One spring afternoon as he and Samuel were working in a field a distance from the cabin, they spotted four men on horseback riding toward them.

"Go and stand by the rifle on the wagon, Peter. Don't pick up the gun, but be ready. If you see me, nod my head."

Peter did as he was told. There were many people hungry and looking for food these days. Also, American militia parties often roamed the country side looting and killing locals if necessary. Peter knew Samuel carried a smaller gun with him all the time.

As they came close enough to hear, the leader of the group shouted, "We are local militia, and we come in peace."

"Where are you from, and what are your names?" asked Samuel.

They men said they lived in the town of Newark and were on their way to St. Davids. They all stated their names, and Samuel recognized them as locals. Samuel then called Peter to come and join them and introduced him as his son.

The men began to tell of the Americans gathering near the fort and across the river from the fort. Everyone felt there would be an attack very soon. The Americans had been successful in several lake battles, and now were more confident about winning the war. They had even attacked Fort York across the lake and drove the British regulars, Canadian militia, and First Nation allies back, allowing the Americans to destroy Fort York and burn the government buildings. Many soldiers were killed or captured. Supplies were taken, including cannons that were to come across the lake to defend Fort George.

"The British are looking for recruits to bolster their forces, so do not be surprised if they come and make you part of the Canadian militia. A young, strong lad like your son would be a good candidate," said the leader of the group. "You will not have a choice. Even you, Samuel, could be taken to fight. It does not matter about your wife and other children."

The men then discussed a few other things, bid their farewell, and left.

"I do not like the sound of this," said Samuel. "We should finish up here and go back to the house to Hannah and the children. It is not a good time for us to be living here as Hannah is now expecting another child in the fall. She cannot be left alone."

That night after the two younger children were in bed, Samuel, Hannah, and Peter talked about what they should do. Samuel did not think fighting was the answer to anything and so would refuse to fight even it meant going to prison. Peter did not want to fight either but did not think prison was a place he wanted to be.

Hannah liked her life here in the little cabin but finally suggested, "Maybe we will have to leave and go farther to the west to get away from the fighting."

For a long time, no one spoke as each thought about the changes it would make in their lives. Samuel had seen his parents leave their country and start over in a new land with nothing but the things they could carry. It had been a great hardship especially for his mother as they had left his father behind in jail.

Hannah's family as well were Loyalists who left everything behind to start over in a new land. Peter, of course, had experienced starting over just a few years ago. As much as they all knew how hard it would be, together they decided to pack up all they could and move to the west. Samuel would try to sell his farm to the neighbor, giving him some cash to purchase land elsewhere. They decided to try and leave in a month as waiting until the crops were harvested would be too late. They needed to be settled and have some sort of shelter before winter and before the new baby arrived.

That night in the loft, Peter could hear Hannah softly crying and Samuel trying to comfort her. Peter thought about his parents leaving, Hannah dying, and now starting another new life with his new family. Would he ever be happy and settle in one spot? He did not know the answer.

*   *   *

Marilee awoke with a start. She looked at the clock, and it said 4:00 a.m. She looked across the bed, and Phillip was sleeping soundly. She looked at the dresser and noticed somewhat of a glow to it. She also just felt as though someone was watching her. This was a whole new experience.

"Hannah," she whispered.

The light glowed a bit brighter and then dimmed.

"Were you listening to my dream?"

Again, the light got brighter.

"Do you know where Peter is now?"

The light remained at the same level of brightness.

"I am going up to the attic to sit for a while. Are you coming with me?"

The light was brighter for a few seconds, and then it disappeared.

Marilee grabbed her housecoat and slippers and the flashlight and closed the bedroom door behind her. She thought it best not to wake Phillip.

As she climbed the stairs to the attic using only the flashlight, she noticed that a glow had appeared in the room above. This was spooky and exciting all at the same time. Marilee kept taking deep breaths to keep calm, but her heart felt like it was going explode in her chest.

At the top of the stairs, Marilee stopped. Across the room sitting by the window, she saw a young girl dressed in dark ragged clothing, but instead of being a solid figure, she was transparent and had a white phosphorescent glow around her. Her hair was disheveled; twigs and leaves stuck to her skirt, and her face was smudged with dirt. Her eyes had a darkness to them but seemed to look right through things.

Was this what a ghost looked like? Marilee then whispered, "Are you Hannah?"

A weak horse voice answered, "Yes."

Marilee felt it best to ask easy questions at first.

"How old are you, Hannah?"

"I am fourteen."

"Have you seen Peter lately?"

"No. He was here once, but he did not stay, and he did not see me."

"Is anyone from your family here in the house?"

"No, but my father is here for a short time."

"Do you know why you are still here?"

"Not really. I know I am dead."

Marilee noticed with each answer the glowing around Hannah was beginning to fade. She didn't know for sure, but maybe it took too much energy to answer questions to a mortal.

"You must be getting tired, so would you like me to tell you all I know about Peter and your family?"

"Yes, please."

Marilee then told Hannah how her family were safe at her uncle's farm, and Peter was staying for the moment at Uncle Samuel's farm.

"Because of the war, he has changed his name to Van Every and is living there as Samuel and Hannah's son. They fear if it becomes known that Peter's family went back to America, he would be considered a traitor as well. Samuel and his family, however, are considering moving farther west toward the end of the lake. It is felt the Americans will attack the town of Newark and the fort very soon."

"Will Peter come back here to be with me?"

"I do not think it is safe for him to be back here right now because of the fighting. Your father may be called to be part of the Canadian militia before the fighting starts again. Your mother is safe with William and Elizabeth, and your brother and sister are safe as well. Your brother can sometimes see you here at the house, and it makes him sad. He and Peter are friends now, and Peter told him you two were going to get married. Andrew told Peter he can see you, and he knows you can see him, but he has not told anyone else. Do you know why I live here in this house, Hannah?"

"No."

"My name is Marilee, and my husband Phillip and I bought this house because we love the historical background and the fact that your family settled here so long ago. It is over two hundred years since you died during the war. We have many people who come and stay here while they are visiting the area. My friend Julie and I feed them breakfast, and then they enjoy the many things to see around here. Sometimes they think it might be fun to see a spirit like yourself while they are here, but we try to discourage it. They mean no harm to you, so do not be afraid of odd-looking things and outfits you do not understand."

"Oh."

"Has some of this information helped you know what's going on?"

"I think so."

"I see it is getting light out, so I need to go and begin getting breakfast ready for the guests we have in the house today. I will come back and chat with you another time."

"Thank you."

Marilee noticed the glow had almost disappeared, and the vision of the young girl was gone now, so she got up from the rocking chair and went down the stairs to the other world she belonged to. This had been a strange experience bridging the gap between two dimensions. The big question was should she tell anyone about the encounter?

Marilee and Julie were quite practiced at working together in the kitchen. It was going into the second season now for Julie, and she truly was a godsend to Loyalist House. Julie seemed to know exactly what Marilee planned to use for serving dishes, for garnishes, and the timing of the different courses. She also knew Marilee's personality, and this morning, she noticed that she was very quiet.

"Is something bothering you this morning, Marilee?"

"Oh. I hoped you wouldn't notice, and then I would not have to tell you."

"Well, you are going to have to tell me now as I am very curious and probably can't work efficiently unless I know."

"OK. I actually saw Hannah this morning and talked to her after I found her in our bedroom watching me early this morning."

Julie almost dropped the whole bowl of eggs to be scrambled on the floor.

"Wow. You have to explain now."

Marilee told her about today's encounter in the attic and about the earlier time with the doll.

"How can you keep this to yourself? I would be bursting if I couldn't tell someone that kind of information."

"I never know how it will be received. People might think I am crazy."

"Well, you can always tell me or Jeannie as we know the background. What are you going to do about her now?"

"I don't know. I know that Peter did not come back, and he did marry someone, but how do I tell her that without upsetting her?"

"Good question. We will have to think about that."

They continued to think about the answer as they served breakfast. Fortunately, the two couples visiting were friends and had their own conversations going on during breakfast. After the kitchen was cleaned up, Marilee phoned Jeannie and asked her to come for coffee.

"Julie, you better stay for coffee and help us come up with an answer. You're involved now."

Julie was delighted to be included.

Jeannie arrived, and she knew right away something was up because both Julie and Marilee kept giving each other an odd look while putting the coffee on the table. Finally, they told her the whole story, and Jeannie once again was speechless.

"This not having anything to say is becoming a habit," teased Marilee.

"And you keep coming up with these crazy experiences."

"I do admit that," said Marilee. "Now we need to decide what our next step is and how we are going to tell Hannah the truth."

"I think we need to find out where Samuel settled if and when he and his family went west. It may mean a road trip to the Hamilton area to check out property data records after the war. There must be museums there that have records."

"Good idea," said Julie. "You two can go someday, and I can hold the fort here with the guests."

Marilee picked up her calendar and looked at some possible dates as the three women chatted over coffee.

Phillip had been working in the office in the Barn lately and helping when it got busy in the tasting room. Today was not too busy, and he was working on numbers for the new project. He was deep in thought when Dave came in.

"The inspector has arrived to look at the revised electrical work, and I thought you might want to be there."

"Of course, I do. Let's go."

When they arrived at the new building, Mike was following the inspector around watching carefully as measurements were recorded. He knew everything was now exactly to code, so this inspection should pass.

At the conclusion, the inspector waited awhile as though he was thinking hard what to say. "I'm not sure of a few things. We may need to redo two areas."

Mike almost exploded. "What areas, and why? Let me see the numbers you wrote down and compare them to what I saw on your tape measure."

The inspector was surprised at the response and began to say how several outlets were not the right distance to be approved.

Mike interrupted, "Show me which ones, and show me the measurements."

The inspector tried to argue that he was correct, and he did not have to show his work, but Dave and Phillip walked over to join them, and he then relented and said he would remeasure.

The remeasuring was done, and the numbers were compared. Mike had the same number as the tape showed, but the inspector had consistently changed each one by four inches.

The three men stood tall looking at the inspector waiting for an answer.

"I must have been confused when I wrote those numbers."

"Then we can expect this inspection to pass, and we can proceed from here?" asked Mike.

They watched as the inspector sheepishly changed the incorrect measurements to the correct ones and initialed the changes.

He began closing his book when Dave said, "You didn't sign the release."

"I was going to do it later."

"Now would be a good time in front of witnesses," said Mike.

He signed the form and gave the men their copy and quickly left without any further conversation.

"There's no doubt in my mind who is behind delaying our project," said Dave. "I have heard a few rumors, and I think I may just do a bit of research on crop production over at Fox Hollow."

Phillip and Mike looked puzzled but figured Dave must know something they didn't.

The rest of the morning was spent arranging for the crews to come in and begin finishing the interior of the production center. Hopefully, they could make up the lost time and be ready in September to begin turning grapes into wine.

MAY

Marilee was worried about this weekend. Loyalist House was fully booked for the next two weeks, and several of the first time guests were asking questions about a ghost in the house. Apparently after happy hour on the Friday, the regulars had informed the new guests about spirits living in the house. One had even asked outright, while Phillip was pouring wine, if Hannah still lived in the attic. Phillip was quite cool and played the "not everyone can see this dimension" card so no one would get spooked.

However, Marilee knew that this was the month that the town had been taken over by the Americans in 1813, and Hannah seemed to be identifying with that year for some reason. The last time there was a major event in the war timeline; Hannah was very active and did manage to scare the guests. She hoped that would not happen again especially since all the guests were now talking about it.

The first night everything was quiet, but when Marilee went to bed on the Saturday night, she fell asleep instantly as she was tired, and then the dreams began.

*　*　*

William Van Every was working close to the barn when he saw a figure approaching. It was definitely a man and the walk looked somewhat familiar. William watched, and when he could distinguish some features, he realized it was his brother David. They both ran the final short distance and embraced in a long bear hug. A man of smaller stature might have been crushed.

"My brother, what are you doing here at my farm? We did not know you would be coming. Is the war over?"

"No, unfortunately, it is only escalating. I have been called back to the militia and must report in two or three days. Some British came past our farm a few days ago and told us to report by the end of the week or earlier. I decided to walk past your farm, even though it is out of the way. I want to see Sarah and the children and you before I go back. I need to talk to you before I see Sarah though."

"What is it, David? Is something wrong?"

"Well, I hope not, but I would like to know that Sarah would be taken care of if anything happens to me. The rumor is the Americans have become quite aggressive and are planning to attack the fort at the village. They have a large amount of fire power and men. If anything happens to me, I would like you to take over the farm on the river and either move there or sell it. You keep the money, and please provide for Sarah and the children. I have written up the papers and brought the necessary documents in case you need them."

"You should not talk like that as it might be tempting fate."

"It is better to be prepared. I have seen some tragic scenes on the battlefield. There have been wives searching for their husbands, hoping they were only injured but finding them dead. In almost all cases, the women and children were left with nothing and no rights to the family property, only some household possessions."

"You can count on me, brother, to take care of Sarah and the children and resolve the farm issue. I do think Elizabeth has enjoyed having Sarah with us."

Just then, the cabin door opened, and Andrew looked over and saw his father. His arrival was not a secret anymore as he shouted, "Father!" And he ran across the yard to greet him.

The shouting, of course, brought the women to the door, and then everyone was running, hugging, crying, and all talking at once. Sarah could not let go of David and found it hard to talk because of a lump in her throat.

Over the next few hours, the stories were told, the questions were asked, but not many answers were found. It was truly a bittersweet moment.

Sarah was so happy to see and hold David, but she knew it was only for a short time, and that made her sad. She was proud that he was fighting for their country but angry that the fighting was taking place in their backyard. Mostly, she worried that something would happen to him, and she would lose another member of the family she loved so much.

The oil in the lamp burned late into the night as the adults and Andrew sat up late discussing, remembering and dreaming of better times.

Early next morning after breakfast, Elizabeth packed food for David, while he and Sarah spent a few precious last minutes together. The family all stood together in the small cabin and prayed for safety and guidance over their time away from each other. Final farewells were said through tears, and David walked toward the village of Newark and danger.

*   *   *

Marilee was so sad when she woke up the next morning, almost as much as when she realized Hannah had been shot while waiting for Peter. She was relieved, however, that no ghostly encounters had taken place in the night.

The nights during the next week were thankfully quiet, and the days very busy. Building at the winery was well under way, and no roadblocks had been thrown up lately. The next big hurdle was going to be the final inspection scheduled for the end of the month. Dave had suggested to Phillip and Mike he was onto some big news about Fox Hollow, and he wanted it solved before the inspection. He asked Phillip for the name of the detective who helped during the problems with the dig.

"Why do we need the police?" asked Mike.

"I'm pretty sure they can help us resolve any further problems we have with Fox Hollow. As well, it might solve some of their cases as well."

Dave wouldn't say anything else, leaving Phillip and Mike looking at each other wondering what he was up to.

"We will just have to trust him," said Phillip.

It was two weeks later, and again, the B&B was full for the weekend. Marilee was feeling nervous and worried again, for if Hannah had reason to become agitated, this would the weekend. The guests this weekend were all new to Loyalist House and were keen to visit as many historical and wine-related spots as possible. There were no questions of spirits in the house but lots about wines. Phillip had everyone captivated at happy hour with his tales of building a winery and offering different tastings.

Today, he had a bottle of last year's sauvignon blanc.

Marilee had decided a few months ago to delete the spot on their website where guests could add comments about their stay. This was just an open invitation for remarks about Hannah. The only way for Hannah's presence, good or bad, to be known now was word of mouth.

That night at bed time, Marilee said a somewhat different prayer for peace and quiet. "Dear Lord. Please let Hannah see what is happening in her world and her families, but let her be calm and accepting of any occurrences in the battle at the fort and the surrounding area."

Marilee had never been someone who believed in the power of prayer, but her involvement with this house and Hannah was beginning to change her thinking.

*   *   *

It was late May 1813, and the residents of the small town of Newark were watching as more American troops were gathering on the lake and across the river at Fort Niagara. The British were still defending the town and Fort George, but their numbers were no match for the Americans.

Fort George, a short distance south on the river, had lost their cannons, and the new ones had been captured in a fight at York earlier in the year, and the British and the Americans were all aware of this fact.

Hannah was in her usual place watching the river for Peter, even though she knew he was elsewhere. It was just after daybreak when she heard the cannons and mortars being fired somewhere down the river. The noise continued all day, and that night, the glow from the burning fort could be seen down the river.

Hannah was worried about her father. She knew he had returned to the militia to fight, but she did not know where he was. All night she paced the house looking toward the river and to the west in the direction of Uncle William's farm, but she could not see anyone. She was so annoyed she thought of tearing the house apart again, but then she remembered the nice lady who also lived there. Maybe she would ask her what happened the next time she saw her. Instead, she sat by the window and sobbed as she was lonely tonight and missed Peter.

Two days later as she watched the river again, she heard more gunfire. This time, she decided to look toward Uncle Samuel's farm. Maybe she would see Peter. She was surprised to find no one at the farm at all and horrified to see troops marching just north of his farm and heading toward the town. The ones marching were wearing blue, and the men running away were wearing red uniforms and regular clothing. Now she was really worried. Had the men found Peter and her uncle and family and killed them or had they been able to escape? How would she find out?

Hannah then forgot about everything else and returned to her old ways. She flew down the stairs and ran up and down the hall making her high-pitched scream as she went. She once again knocked pieces of furniture over, and lamps fell crashing to the ground.

Suddenly, two doors in the hall opened, and a person not dressed like her came out. Hannah sort of remembered this had happened before, but she couldn't remember how it ended, so she just stood there and screamed.

*　*　*

The guests were horrified as well and just stood and stared. It was somewhat of a standoff, and who knows how long it would have lasted if Marilee and Phillip hadn't arrived on the scene.

"It's all right, everyone. If you wish to join Phillip downstairs in the living room, he will explain everything." Marilee was almost yelling when she realized Hannah's screaming had stopped, and there was no sign of her anywhere.

After the guests had retreated downstairs, Marilee opened the attic door and climbed the stairs. The room was not messed up this time, which was a plus, but she did not see any sign of Hannah.

"Hannah, I know you must be upset, but if you wish, I can stay and talk to you about what has happened."

A dim light appeared by the window, and the figure of the forlorn girl appeared as it had the last time.

"Do you want to tell me what you saw that upset you?"

"Yes. I think Peter and Uncle Samuel's family are dead and maybe my father as well."

Marilee then explained how the fort had been burned, and two days later, the town had been invaded, and the Americans now occupied the town. The fighting had taken place close to Uncle Samuel's farm, but they were not hurt. They decided to move farther west before the fighting began.

"I do not know about your father, but I will check into it and see if we can find where he went."

How Marilee could know all this amazed Hannah. How did she find this out? Was she a ghost too? Mostly, though, Hannah was pleased to find out Peter was alive. Maybe he would still come back to her.

The next morning at breakfast, the guests had more questions, and Marilee and Julie answered as best they could. No one seemed upset or wanted to leave, so hopefully all would be quiet tonight.

Phillip commented, "I may have to try and get a discount on scotch if this keeps up."

JUNE

Samuel and Hannah Van Every, with the help of Peter, loaded as much as they dare onto the wagons, hitched up the oxen team and the horse Samuel had purchased, and began their journey west to hopefully a safer life. It was hard to decide what to take and what to leave. The farm was sold to a neighbor who wanted more land and who was not worried about the possibility of Americans taking over.

Peter had spent the month before they left literally in hiding. There seemed to be more men stopping at the farm on their way to and from the village. There were British and Canadian militia and First Nations warriors all on their way to protect the fort. Mostly, they were hungry and wanted food, but several of the British soldiers asked if there were any other men on the property who should be fighting.

Samuel and Peter had created a hiding spot for Peter between the roof and the overhang of the barn. It was a tight space, but Peter could access it quickly, and no one would think to look there. The trick was always being able to hide before any visitors saw him working around the farm. He was getting quite good at doing the inside chores, but he missed the fresh air. There were a few close calls, but Samuel was not only tall; he could be very forceful when he spoke to someone.

Samuel was exempt from fighting as he had suffered an injury while working on the farm and did walk with a slight limp. At times, however, the limp could become more pronounced if the situation required it to be.

Samuel decided they would take two wagons as it would be easier to settle and build if he had his equipment with him. He would leave most of the animals except the horse and the oxen team. On one wagon, he loaded all the farm implements he would need.

At this stage of their life, he did have duplicates, but he figured one scythe, one rake, and one plow would do for now. Since he had Peter to help with the journey, he knew he had an extra driver.

Samuel had built three wooden crates to pack everything they would take. He had modified the wagon with blocks to hold the crates firmly in place as they traveled over the rough terrain. Samuel and Peter had also built a cover for the one wagon for protection from the weather and to protect the children and Hannah from the sun. They had made metal hoops to attach to the side of one wagon and had taken cloth and oiled it to make it waterproof. It looked like a combination covered wagon and a sailing vessel.

Hannah, his wife, was busy with the two small children and found packing difficult, not only because of distractions but also she had to decide what to take and what to leave. She knew that she could never leave behind the household goods that had been passed down through the family. They represented the past and the struggles the Loyalist families had endured the first time they were forced to leave a country because of political strife.

She also had managed to collect some efficient kitchen equipment over the past few years. The reflective oven that quickened cooking time was truly helpful, especially with small children. Her butter churn and pickling crocks were also some of her prized possessions.

Not knowing their new location made the packing more difficult. Their future home might not be near a general store that sold goods or be near a blacksmith who could make simple metal pieces to make household chores easier. Her favorite metal hooks fashioned by the blacksmith to hold pots over the fire fortunately would be easy to pack.

The family really only had two sets of clothing with extra garments for cold weather. There were two blankets for each person and mattresses that could be used in the wagon on the journey. Their clothes would be used to wrap breakable items, although there were not many breakable things in their home.

Hannah thought back to when her parents had fled on foot the Americas and returned to a British colony with only the clothes they wore and a few possessions they could carry. There had been no wagons or animals or specially crafted crates. She knew she was one of the lucky ones.

The day came to leave, and as sad as it was, they all knew it was for the best. The plan was to travel within site of the lake but far enough away not to be seen. It was just midmorning when they realized this was not a wise plan. They could see several ships flying the American flag sailing east on the lake and at times had to stop in the woods to avoid meeting soldiers also traveling the same way.

By noon, the small group of pioneers were heading more south then west. Samuel knew the way to several British posts in the area but decided to avoid those as well. He knew it would take several extra days, but he felt traveling closer to Lake Erie would be a better plan. After reaching Stoney Creek, they would continue west again.

The roads were very rough, and most of the spots they traveled were barely passable paths for a man walking, let alone a wagon pulled by oxen. Samuel often had to walk in front of the team with his scythe to cut brush down to make it passable. It would be a slow journey.

The first night, they found a spot to rest located near a stream and a much larger stand of trees. There was water for the animals and protection for the wagons. As much as Samuel thought it was safe, he and Peter took turns over night, keeping watch over the site.

The morning arrived after an uneventful night. Samuel figured they had traveled about ten or more miles which meant it would take at least five days to arrive at their destination. On the second day of journey, they came across a path that had recently been used by someone. There were many footprints, hoof prints, and wheel tracks all going toward the river and the fort.

Samuel realized the militia had traveled through here, but he did not know which side. Thank goodness the militia were going the opposite direction and had passed this way earlier.

Hannah was sitting back in the wagon with the children, so he made no comment to her, but he did give Peter a keep-your-eyes-open look as he pointed to the ground.

It was a clear sunny day, and the humidity increased as they continued. When they stopped for a break near a stream, Samuel said, "We need to find a protected spot tonight as I think it may rain by the look of the sky." They all agreed to stop early if they came across the right spot.

It was late afternoon when Peter spied a cluster of buildings about a mile ahead down in a valley. "Look up ahead. I think it may be a small farm. Do you think the farmer might let us stay near his farm for the night?"

"It is a possibility," replied Samuel. "You stay here with the others, and I will walk down and ask."

Peter got down from the covered wagon and gave the reins to Hannah. He then walked over to the team of oxen to keep them from following Samuel. They were gentle beasts and would normally have stayed still, but they had been following Samuel for the last two days and did begin to follow him as he descended toward the farm.

As they watched from the top of the hill, they could see what transpired but could only guess at the conversation. As Samuel was halfway down the hill, a figure emerged from the barn carrying a gun. Samuel stopped and raised his hands to show he was not carrying a gun with him. The two men were now face to face talking, and Hannah noticed the stranger had lowered his gun to his side. Samuel and Peter did exactly the same thing when a stranger had come to the farm. Shortly, the farmer and Samuel began walking up the hill toward the two wagons.

Samuel spoke first, "This is Mr. Johnston. Sir, this is my wife, Hannah, and my three children, Peter, Elizabeth, and Thomas."

"Pleased to meet you. I am sorry I cannot offer you a place in my home for the night, but you are welcome to stay in the barn. There is water for your animals, and I think we can put one wagon in the upper part of the barn as I have no hay in there yet. It looks like rain tonight. Please join my family for supper meagre as it may be."

Hannah and Samuel thanked the kind man and prepared to take the wagons slowly down the hill. Mr. Johnston walked in front of the horse holding his bridle while Peter directed the horse with the reins. The oxen lumbered down the hill holding back the wagon with their strength. Once they were safely at the bottom, Mr. Johnston went in to find his wife. She came out of the cabin followed by five children that looked like stair steps all under the age of about seven or eight. Introductions were made, and after a few moments of shyness, the children were all playing together.

The rest of the afternoon was spent taking care of the animals and putting the covered wagon in the hay loft. Supper was a delicious meal made from combining their food supplies. The two families carried on conversations easily with one another while the children played. Of course, the topic was the war, and Mr. Johnston explained how, just three days ago, the British militia had stopped at his farm on their way to Fort George. Samuel told him what he knew about the latest battles and what everyone expected to happen next.

Mr. Johnston then explained to Samuel about a route he should take to avoid both trouble and bad trails. He had gone this way about a year ago, and it seemed passable.

Both families turned in for the night, and the Van Every family felt quite comfortable with their accommodations. Before going to bed, they all prayed, thanking the Lord for their good fortune in finding this family and a safe resting spot.

The next morning, everyone worked together to hitch up the wagons and get on their way. The children would have liked to spend the day playing with their new friends, but the journey must continue. Both families knew they had made a good friend, even though neither would probably meet again. Goodbyes were said, and Samuel and his family continued west through the valley.

Mr. Johnston had been right about the path through the valley. It was a good trail and followed the river. Samuel was a little concerned, though, as he felt everyone probably knew this was a good path so there would be a greater chance of meeting someone. Fortunately, today was not a traveling day for others, and the young family made it to a perfect resting spot for the night. Again, they had water, protection, and privacy in the woods. God indeed was watching over them on the trip.

The next two days went as the past three. The rain was just a sprinkle, the paths, though rough, were easy to follow, and the sun going down in the west was an excellent compass.

On the fifth day, they came upon the settlement of Ancaster. Its location advantage was the stream cascading down the escarpment allowing the water power to run a mill. The mill had been built almost thirty years prior to Samuel and Hannah's journey. Farmers around the area brought their grain there to be ground into flour, thus creating a thriving but small community. This would be where the Van Every family would settle.

Samuel went first to the records office and inquired about land to be purchased. With the money from the sale of his Niagara property, he was able to purchase one hundred acres of uncleared land below the escarpment with some money left over for building. It would mean starting from scratch again, but he and Hannah had discussed this and were willing to try.

After one more night camping in a livery stable, Samuel and Hannah reached their new property to begin a new life. Hopefully, this place would be free from strife and war.

Pioneer life was difficult, but resources were abundant. Peter and Samuel decided to keep some of the fields of grass to use as hay for the winter. They planted some late barley, very late in the season, and hoped it would give them a small crop. There were lots of trees to cut for lumber for the buildings, but since time was an issue, they decided on a small log cabin. When Peter wasn't helping raise log walls, he took the oxen and gathered stones for a fireplace. By the end of October, Samuel was able to complete the cabin with a large fireplace for cooking and a bread oven for baking. Their new neighbors and friends had all helped to build the cabin. This certainly was a caring community.

Hannah helped as much as she was able, but the daily chores of fetching water from the stream and cooking meals over the outdoor fire took its toll on her body. At the end of July, she gave birth to a baby boy, but he was too young and too small to survive. It was a sad time in the Van Every home, but with a strong faith, they managed to keep going, knowing their future and their children's future would be better.

Deciding to bring many pieces of iron from their previous home had been a wonderful idea. They did not have to find a blacksmith and wait for him to make the pieces for them. When winter arrived in November, they were warm, had blankets and mattresses, excellent cooking facilities, and still had some food supplies. They were sleeping on the floor, but Samuel felt he would be able to make a bed for himself and Hannah over the winter months.

Peter enjoyed this time working with Samuel but always in the back of his mind, he knew he wanted more than staying on his new father's farm. He had originally wanted to farm the Gillham farm on the river, but a war had changed his plans. He knew he should be grateful for the life Samuel and Hannah had provided for him. But at some point, he knew he would have to move on. He had heard that the city of York was filled with opportunities. It couldn't be that far away. He would keep thinking, but he would remain with the Van Everys until the farm was running well, a barn was built, and maybe by then young Thomas would be able to help his father.

*   *   *

The work on the winery had been amazing. The new wine production center and bottling facility was completed inside, and the landscapers were giving it that road appeal that everybody talked about. The final inspection was scheduled for the last day of the month. If all went well, the grand opening would be mid-July.

Phillip was in the office when Dave walked in with the local paper.

"Did you see this Phillip?"

"No. I haven't had time to read it yet."

Dave opened the paper to page six and put it on the desk.

Phillip scanned it and kept saying "whoa" as he read.

Dave then described how he had taken a walk over to Fox Hollow woods one day and found an area fenced off with high shrubs around the perimeter. "I couldn't get inside the fence, but when I got right up close, I found the new crop they are growing— marijuana. I had been suspicious as I had seen lights back there at night. But I took pictures with my cell phone and then went and visited Detective Barrens. He was thrilled to get the photo as they had been suspicious, but short of using a helicopter, they were unable to get in there to look.

"I have given them permission to go through the back of our place today to get there as long as they don't destroy the vines. You better tell Marilee so she doesn't get upset and call the police."

"So what happens to Fox Hollow?" asked Phillip.

"Well, I think they may have a paid vacation coming up in a while. The town is considering canceling, not only their winery license but also their B&B permit. They don't look fondly on that sort of thing."

"I surmise that's why we were running into so much interference every time we wanted to do something," said Phillip.

"Probably. He knew we were too close and could find out. I think they were about ready to harvest it in the next few days, so my timing was good. The town have been concerned about the increase of the amount of pot the local teens have been buying. They may be the source."

"This is good news, but who would ever have thought something like that could be going on in this staid conservative community?"

"I'm sure it will be the talk of the town. Are we ready for the inspection on Thursday?"

Phillip showed him the checklist he was keeping of work to be finished before the inspection. They only had some minor plumbing work to do, and the men were coming in today to finish it. "We should be."

All went well the rest of the week, and on Thursday the inspectors came, looked at everything, and signed off on the building. The winery production center was ready for business.

JULY

Summer was here. The tourists were back; the fruit festivals all provided the entertainment expected, and it was one of the best seasons ever for fruit production. Loyalist House Winery held their grand opening, and every winery owner in the district came to enjoy the celebration with the exception of Fox Hollow.

As for the B&B season, the bookings for the summer were greater than other years. At least a third of the guests were repeats from the first two seasons. Marilee and Phillip figured they must be doing something right. Phillip's only concern was the need to come up with more riveting stories for his happy hour crowd who had heard all the others. He figured he may have to make a list to keep track of who had heard what.

Marilee was still concerned about Hannah, but lately, there had only been sobbing in the attic which probably could not be heard by the guests. She and Jeannie had gone to Hamilton and looked up some records of property owners and did find that Samuel Van Every had owned land in the Ancaster region and had stayed there until he died. It did not list Peter Van Every as owning land there after Samuel died. They both wondered if Peter had gone to York.

* * *

Hannah had once again been watching by the river and sobbing. She noticed troops both on the road and on the river, all going south. She decided the best way to find out was to look toward Uncle William's house, and maybe she would overhear something being said.

Lunch was over, and William and Andrew were sitting inside to avoid the midday heat. Sarah and Elizabeth were taking a short break as well before they began the chores needing to be done before the day ended. They were all enjoying a moment of relaxation and talking when someone outside began banging on the door frightening everyone inside. Three men stood on the step, and when William opened the door, they walked right into the center of the small cabin. Sarah and Elizabeth gathered the wide-eyed children behind their skirts protecting them from possible harm.

"What do you want?" asked William.

"We were just passing by and wanted to tell you what has happened in the town," said the man dressed in overalls. "The Americans invaded the town in May and are occupying it now. Most of the men that were still in town at the time were arrested and are in jail. The others must carry their parole papers with them at all times and produce them if asked by the soldiers patrolling the streets. It is not a pleasant time for anyone. There have even been occasions where they have pushed our women out of the way to get their business done first."

Sarah looked horrified and was almost afraid to ask but managed, "Where are all the British militia and our local men who are fighting with them?"

"They apparently retreated after several days of fighting to St. Davids and Queenston. There is supposed to be some fighting going on near there right now. But I have not heard any details."

The other two men stood beside their friend shaking their heads in agreement but did not utter a word.

Elizabeth asked, "How long is this war going to continue? Will all this land become part of America?"

"No one knows how long it will last, but as Loyalists, we hope the Americans will leave soon."

Timidly, Sarah asked, "Will it be safe to go back to our houses on the river?"

Kindly, the spokesman said, "I venture that is the least safe place of all, except for right in town."

This was not what anyone wanted to hear. Sarah went behind the curtained wall as she did not want these strangers seeing her cry. Elizabeth looked at William and gave him a silent message. William then asked the men to come to the barn as he had some other questions to ask. The group of men, including Andrew, left the cabin and walked to the barn.

When they were out of range from the cabin, William asked, "When local men are killed, does anyone notify the families, and what is done with the bodies?"

"Unfortunately, the bodies are usually left on the battlefield until families come looking for them. If the battle has been in favor of the British, after it is safe, soldiers do come and carry the bodies back to be buried, most likely in a common grave. We can assume the enemy does the same thing. It is not a pretty picture. Do you have family that is fighting?"

"Yes, my brother is fighting with the British. He was ordered by them to fight. And a few weeks ago, he came by here on his way to Newark as they suspected there would be an invasion. His family is living with us as it was not safe along the river."

"There were casualties, but we do not know any numbers. The only way to know would be to find a British officer and ask if they knew. It is very frustrating for families right now. If you give us his name and we have an opportunity to inquire, we will. We are on our way to Fort Erie, and if we return this way, we will stop."

"Thank you," said William. "Is there anything I can help you with for your journey?"

"We just need some water for our canteens and maybe some fresh bread, please."

"That we can do."

Hannah was quite interested to hear all this. She also wanted to know where her father was. She hoped he was in St. Davids which was not far away. Maybe he would stop in on his way by. She would wait.

Hannah waited for what seemed like a long time, but she had no concept of time anymore. Her father did not return to the house as he had in the past. What she did see was the bright glow of a fire to the south. It must have been large as the sky was very bright orange. It stayed that way all night, and the next morning in daylight, smoke could be seen rising in the same spot.

One night as Hannah was sitting by the window in the attic, she had a strange sensation that someone was watching her. She looked around and did not see the nice lady who lived there. She wished she could remember her name, but she really had trouble concentrating sometimes. She felt the presence more than saw it. It was a man, and he looked quite filmy and transparent. At first, she was frightened, but she heard a voice she recognized, saying, "Come with me, Hannah, it is time to go."

She suddenly realized it was her father, but why was it time to go and where? Before she could answer, he was gone. She traveled quietly around the house looking for him, but he was not there. Why did he not stay with her in their house? Had he gone to get her mother? Why was he so transparent? Was he dead? Did she look like that? How would she ever find out all these answers? She went back to the attic, sat by the window, and watched and sobbed for a long time.

*   *   *

AUGUST

One afternoon when all the prep and cleanup for the B&B were done, Marilee was cleaning out some outdated books and magazine from a shelf in the living room. At the bottom of the pile was the family history book given to her by a descendent of the Van Every family. She had almost forgotten this was where she left it the last time she looked at it. She sat down and began to read it again, and for some reason, she started at the back of the book. She knew she had read the whole book, but she could not remember the part she was reading now. The pages were partly stuck together and were written on different paper with a different typewriter. This was all new information. Someone had written about Peter.

It told about him returning and eventually living with Samuel as his son, but she already knew that from her dreams and her research at the church. It was the next part that was interesting.

That night, Marilee had a dream that gave her the much needed information.

*   *   *

Peter enjoyed working on the farm with Samuel. They had built the small cabin, completed the barn, and were able to harvest a small crop. Where they had located was a friendly community. People helped each other, and they cared for one another if someone was sick. When Hannah had lost the baby, a neighbor came to the house to help her. Another neighbor took the two young children for three days so Hannah could recover. Peter knew Samuel and Hannah would survive quite nicely in this community.

But the feeling for adventure was always in the back of Peter's mind. He heard of opportunities near York. He had even scouted out other young men in the community who could come and replace him on the farm so Samuel would not be left without help. One day at the end of August, Peter approached Samuel and told him of his dreams of owning his own farm.

"I feel I owe you a great debt for accepting me as family, but I would like to have a job where I could save my own money and buy a farm, get married, and raise a family. You and Hannah have been a great inspiration to me. You work hard, you love your children, and you are kind to everyone. I would like to follow that example, but I must do it on my own."

"Peter, I am of course saddened to hear you want to leave, but I know everyone must become an adult and live independently. I too left my father's home and started my own life just as you want to. We truly love you as a son and want the best for you. I could not have completed this move without you. Your help has been invaluable. We can only wish you the very best in this next part of your life as I have no money to help you get started."

"No, no. I do not want any money. I will get a job and then earn my own. All I want is your blessing and know that you understand why I have to go."

"We do, Peter, and want you to know you will always be our son. Hannah will be very sad, and the children will miss you after you leave. You must write to us to let us know where you settle."

Peter and Samuel continued to talk about where he would go and how he would make his dreams come true. The most difficult part was telling Hannah and the children that night at supper. There were tears and pleas not to go, but in the end, they all knew it was for the best.

Peter would leave at the end of the week with his few belongings in a sack—a rifle and a small amount of cash that Samuel insisted he take.

It was a sad farewell, but he knew that leaving his new family this time was on better terms than when he left his family across the river. He often wondered what his mother and father were doing in America, and did they know where he was.

By now, Peter was quite adept at traveling on his own and surviving in the wilderness. As it was the end of the summer, the weather was a more moderate temperature, and the biting insects had almost disappeared. There were still berries in the woods, and they had been abundant, so the wild animals were well fed this year.

He knew his path would take him along the other side of the lake, so there would be water and hopefully no militia looking for fights. Compared to his other adventures through wilderness, this one was easy. There were even several taverns along what was considered a road where one could stop for a meal or the night. Peter decided to avoid these as he wanted to save his money for the future.

After three days, he arrived in a small community just north of the lake. He stopped in a store and asked about employment. As luck would have it, the owner did not need any one at the moment, but his brother in York was looking for an assistant to help in his dry goods store. He gave Peter the name and address and a letter introducing Peter.

Peter continued on to York. He was horrified at how built up it was and how many people lived there. There were real streets, though, often muddy and large brick buildings where many people worked.

Mr. Riley, the shopkeeper, greeted Peter and found him to be a very polite young man. He said he would give him a chance for a month to see if this was the right job for him. He even suggested a rooming house where he could find accommodations at a reasonable cost. Peter quickly figured he might have to work for a long time before he could buy property, but at least this was a start.

Peter quickly settled into a routine of hard work during the long days and sometimes lonely nights in his room at the boarding house. Some of his fellow boarders were always trying to persuade him to come to the tavern at nights and have some fun, but Peter knew that would be wasting his money, and they did seem dangerous, as often someone would return with a blackened eye or bloody nose. He was definitely not a city person and just wanted to return to his own property out of the city.

The store was quite a hub of activity, and Peter got to know where everything was and often what certain customers liked. Mr. Riley was pleased with Peter and how he handled himself, and after a month, he hired him on permanently and said he would be receiving a raise after a year. It was hard work, and the only day he had off was Sunday.

While living with Samuel and Hannah, there had been no formal church near their farm; but every Sunday, the small family had gathered together for readings and prayer.

One Sunday while walking, Peter had noticed a large spectacular church not far from his boarding house. The congregation were just leaving after a service. Peter stood and watched from the street until all the people had left. He remained for a while, and the preacher at the door noticed him. He walked to the end of the path and introduced himself. He asked Peter a lot of questions, and Peter in turn asked him many as well.

Before saying goodbye, the minister invited Peter to come to a service on the next Sunday. Peter said he would think about it.

By the next weekend, he had decided it might be a good thing to do. Samuel and Hannah would expect him to become involved in some kind of religious meetings, and it might be a good way to meet people and find out more about the city. Sunday morning, he was up early and ready to go well ahead of schedule. He dressed in his best clothes which now looked a bit shabby, but they would have to do.

As he entered the church, he was quite taken aback. Inside was the largest church he had seen in his life. The woodwork and the carvings were magnificent; there were gold religious pieces everywhere. There was music playing from an instrument he had never heard before, but it was beautiful. As the minister entered, he was followed by several other men and some small boys all dressed in long robes with white surpluses over top. It was very majestic. One expected the King of England to walk in next.

As the service began, Peter realized it was from the same prayer book they had used at the cabin. This must be an Anglican church like the one he had once attended in Newark and where, as a baby, he had been baptized. He felt almost at home, except for the grandeur and the scale of everything.

After the service, a few people said a polite hello; but as he left, he noticed a young lady watching him from across the church. He smiled and hoped his face did not turn a hundred shades of red. He quickly looked away and kept walking. As he walked home, he thought he might go back next week.

Peter was enjoying his new job in the town of York, but he longed for open spaces of farmland. He continued attending St. James church every Sunday and soon began to meet more people.

Saving money was his ultimate goal, but he found he had to spend some so as not to look like a poor farmhand. He resented this mentality but decided he had to play the part. His employer complimented him when he came to work dressed in new clothes. Mr. Riley was giving Peter more chances to work in the store and helping customers now that he knew Peter was worthy of his trust.

One day, the pretty young woman from church entered the store with her mother. Mr. Riley introduced them to Peter.

"Mrs. Barry, this is my new assistant, Peter Van Every. Peter, this is Mrs. Barry and her daughter Agnes."

"How do you do," said Peter.

"Mrs. Barry is a good customer here at the store, and I am sure you will attend to her needs today," added Mr. Riley.

"Yes, sir."

"Have we not seen you at church the past few Sundays?" inquired Mrs. Barry.

"Yes, I have been attending since I moved here a few months ago. Now what can I help you with today?"

Mrs. Barry then gave Peter her list of things she needed for the house, but she continued to ask Peter personal questions about his life the entire time they were collecting the items on the list. Her daughter Agnes barely spoke but followed along behind her mother never taking her eyes off Peter.

As Mrs. Barry was paying her bill, she said to Peter, "We are having a few young people over to our home next week. Could you join us for dinner? I'm sure Mr. Riley does not make you work on Sunday, and we promise not to keep you out late."

She gave Mr. Riley a slight smile and handed Peter a card with her name and address on it.

"Thank you, Mrs. Barry, and it has been a pleasure meeting you both." Peter then looked directly at Agnes and smiled what he hoped was his best smile as he carried the packages out to the carriage waiting to take them home.

Back inside, he was having trouble thinking about anything else other than dinner at the Barry's home. Mr. Riley noticed this and began to tell him about the Barry family.

"Mr. Thomas Barry is a storekeeper and sells clothing and dry goods, which of course we do not. We have a good friendship with the Barrys, and our businesses complement each other. Agnes is their only daughter. They live on George Street, and Mr. Barry is also the town clerk of York. I will tell you an interesting story about Mrs. Barry, but I suggest you do not mention it at dinner. It will explain why they are very protective of their daughter."

"In Ancaster, where your parents have settled, there is a mill built by a James Wilson in 1789. He and his wife had their eight-year-old daughter taken from their home and despite searching found no trace of her existence anywhere. For five years, they mourned her loss. One day, a stranger came to live in town, and when he heard the story, he told Mr. Wilson that it was his understanding that a white child was being held by an Indian band in Newark and would be about thirteen years old.

"As it was winter, Mr. Wilson and his brother hitched up a sleigh, and taking gifts to give the tribe made the two-day trip. They presented their gifts to the tribe, and as the uncle talked and bestowed the gifts, the father's eye took in the attending figures including a white child he recognized to be his daughter. The child gave a flicker of recognition which was enough for them. There are several versions as to what happened next, but the end result was the father grabbing the daughter and everyone racing off in the sleigh, whipping the horses to go faster, and having to beat off a few natives following them.

"The rescue was successful, and the child grew up in Ancaster until she was once again carried off. This time, it was by Mr. Barry who married her and brought her to York as his wife."

Peter was speechless. He did not think things like that really happened, but he did not think Mr. Riley would make up a story like that either.

That week seemed to drag on, but Peter did have several chances to ask Mr. Riley about the etiquette of attending a dinner at someone's home. By Saturday night, they both felt Peter was ready for the big event.

The Barry home was lovely and as grand a home as Peter had ever seen. It was even larger than the Van Every home next door to where he had grown up.

He was introduced to many new people, and he just hoped he could remember their names later. At dinner, the table was set with more cutlery at one place setting than his mother owned all together. It was a good thing this had been one of the things Mr. Riley had talked about. He did have a chance to talk to Agnes, though, as they had been placed beside each other at dinner.

She was not shy and had a lot of questions to ask him. In what seemed like a very short time, the guests began to leave, and Peter was offered a ride home with another family. He had so many new experiences going through his mind it was hard to get to sleep that night. Tonight, living in the town of York did not seem quite as bad and as lonely as before.

Over the next months, Peter remained busy working for Mr. Riley and courting Ms. Agnes Barry. Once Mr. Barry discovered Peter was a Loyalist, he became very fond of him and knew he was the right man for his daughter.

Over the next year and a half, Peter courted Agnes; and in 1816, he asked her to marry him. Mr. and Mrs. Barry were thrilled. The wedding date was set, and Peter sent a letter to William and Sarah inviting them to York for the wedding.

Mrs. Barry knew Peter's parents might feel lost in the city, so she arranged for the whole family to stay with her sister at a house not far away. William and Sarah now had four children so were pleased to be able to stay with someone from the Barry family.

The day arrived, and all was perfect. The war had ended, the city was growing and prospering, and people had put their losses behind them but still honoring their past. Peter and Agnes were truly in love, and their faces reflected their happiness.

Peter tried not to think of where his parents were and if they were as happy as he was. He knew his mother would not be really happy with part of her family gone, but he vowed to write her a letter and try to tell her how happy he and Agnes were.

In 1816, Peter and Agnes were married; and as a wedding present, Mr. Barry presented them with a hundred acres of land in Etobiocke Township that began at the lake and stretched north.

*   *   *

Marilee awoke smiling in the morning. She now knew what happened to Peter. She would like to think the second child was named for her Hannah in Loyalist House, but she would never know. Now that she knew how and where Peter came to live in York, she would tell Hannah the whole story. But the big question was when would she tell her?

SEPTEMBER

The winery was gearing up for harvest season. It had been a wonderful growing season. The vines were loaded with grapes, and the sun just kept shining. It would be a good year once again for Merlots and Rieslings. Dave and Mike were busy organizing workers and farmers and the transportation so it would all come together.

Two days later, the grapes were ready to pick. Dave tested the grapes one morning and found the seeds turning brown and the bricks or sweetness just at the right level. The custom pickers would pick all the whites first and then start on the reds. The whites would be destemmed first and then crushed and pressed immediately. From there, they would be put into the tanks to ferment.

The reds took a bit more work. They would be put into a tank and allowed to ferment for two weeks with skin contact. This, of course, gave them the characteristic color and acidity. Then the grapes were pumped into the press, and the juice went to barrels or tanks.

Once this process was completed, the grapes stayed in the tanks for a year. The tanks always had to be emptied before the harvest started the following year.

Phillip was keeping track of all the numbers, both coming in and going out. The different farms contracted to bring their grapes to Loyalist House had to have their loads weighed so they could be paid. He also had to have all the necessary bottles and tops and cases on hand ready for the bottling process, even though bottling was not being done at this time. It was like a symphony orchestra with every instrument playing something different and hopefully ending at the same time.

September always looked as though it might be a busy month at the B&B, and because most of the guests were seasoned travellers, registrations and breakfasts should run smoothly. However, this month seemed to be filled with glitches in the bookings and peculiar tastes for breakfast.

The second weekend, all the rooms were fully booked for the three nights. On the Saturday afternoon, the doorbell rang, and a young couple with two children were standing at the door with all their luggage and a small dog. Phillip had answered and was surprised to see the group and even more amazed when they announced they were the Petersons and were checking in for one night.

Phillip stammered a bit and said, "Please come in, and I will call my wife."

The group entered the foyer and managed to somehow load all their things into the center of the hall. Fortunately, the dog was on a leash but looked as though it would break free at any moment.

Marilee came down the stairs and was surprised to see the pile of luggage on the floor. Phillip left at that moment and went to the office to retrieve the reservation book to check for their names.

Mr. Peterson gave Marilee all the details and was becoming somewhat disturbed as he realized something about their reservation was amiss.

Marilee began asking all the normal questions about when they booked and who they talked to. When it was revealed all the bookings had been done on the internet, she knew there was a problem.

"We have been booked for this weekend for almost a year as the guests who are here booked last year when they were here."

"But why was I able to book through a group offering special deals at your B&B for Saturday night?" asked Mr. Peterson.

"I'm not sure as we do not work with any group giving special deals. We also never book single weekend nights during the busy season," Marilee went on to explain to the family that pets were not allowed at Loyalist House, and all this information was on the Web site attached to the booking information.

By this time, the younger child was whining, asking when could they swim in the pool; the child holding the dog was letting the leash out, and the dog was into the dining room under the table, and Mrs. Peterson was trying to ignore both the kids and the dog and was looking through her messages on her cell phone.

Marilee made a quick decision and asked if they would like to all go to the patio and resolve the situation. Phillip came back with the log book and said there was no record anywhere of a booking through an agency. As the group left, he put their luggage into a corner in the dining room out of the way of other guests and followed the group to the outside.

Marilee held back after showing the family the directions and began whispering orders to Phillip, "Find out how much he paid and how he paid. This sounds like a scam to me. We will have to find him another place for tonight, but that could be a problem. Don't let that dog loose in the garden. I am getting some lemonade and cookies."

Marilee quickly put the drinks and plastic cups and cookies on a tray to take outside. She then dialed the phone number of the Chamber of Commerce and explained the situation. They said they would look for a room for the night and get back to her. She put the phone on the tray and went to the patio to try and figure out how something like this could happen.

The Petersons, by this time, had explained to Phillip how they were thrilled to find a B&B near Niagara Falls for only one hundred dollars a night, and so they thought it would be a fun spur of the moment weekend. The advertisement they responded to said the B&B had a pool and was pet friendly, so the whole family was looking forward to fun.

Mrs. Peterson then spoke for the first time and announced, "Both the children and I are on gluten-free diets, so we have to stick to our special diets for breakfast."

Marilee was nonplussed that this woman had not yet figured out that her family would not be staying at Loyalist House tonight or ever. She also noticed both children had devoured all the cookies on the plate, and the mother had not said a word to them. Did she not know cookies contained wheat flour and were not gluten free?

Phillip explained how they had probably been conned by some internet scam and might want to consider talking to the police as well as canceling their credit card.

Thankfully, the phone rang, and the Chamber of Commerce had found them a room that met all their needs. It was even closer to Niagara Falls.

Reluctantly, Mr. Peterson rounded up the children and the dog and his wife and proceeded back to the front of the house all the while, hinting about how it would be nice to taste the wine from Loyalist House. Phillip went inside and brought all their luggage to the porch. This way, no one would have to go inside again. He also gave Mr. Peterson a bottle of red wine from the winery.

As the family drove out the lane, Phillip and Marilee breathed a sigh of relief that they had dodged a potential bullet.

"I am going to call Detective Barrens and tell him about this incident. I have the name of the group selling these scams on the internet. I think he might be very interested. As well, I doubt that Mr. Peterson, if that is his name, may not report this," said Phillip.

The rest of the weekend went very smoothly, but Marilee was still amazed about the lack of knowledge people had when it came to knowing about food and allergies.

OCTOBER

Marilee was beginning to breathe a slight sigh of relief as the season was just about over. She was pleased with how well it ran this year and how Julie could take over at any point when she had another commitment. She had decided this fall not to help at the museum as the new winery would take more of her time over the winter than last year. She was also determined to help Hannah either move on or be happy by the end of the year.

There had not been any incidents in the attic lately other than the sobbing which Marilee could hear some nights. She knew she should try and go up to see if Hannah was in the mood for talking, but she still didn't know how to tell her that Peter had married someone else.

She and Jeannie were going to the church for one more try to wrap up who died when in the Van Every family. John was going to be there to meet them this week one day. This had turned into a two-and-a-half-year project finding out about one family. Marilee almost felt like she was part of the family now.

It had been a very busy weekend with a full house, and Marilee was so tired when she went to bed that night she didn't bother to say her evening prayer request for peace from Hannah.

*   *   *

Hannah had been thinking as she sat by the window watching day after day. She was thinking about her father. She was pretty sure now that he was dead and had moved on to another dimension. Hopefully, he went to heaven as he had been a good father. She still had not found an answer as to why he left her behind. She was also thinking about her mother. Did she know he was dead? This made her sad as her mother had already suffered enough, and she was partly to blame.

Hannah suddenly remembered the nice lady from downstairs had told her how Andrew could sometimes see her and the house. Maybe she could get a message to him about their father. She went down to the front of the empty house and looked toward the west and concentrated.

She saw William, Elizabeth, her mother, and the children sitting around the fire. Andrew was sitting at the window looking out, even though it was dark. She looked directly at Andrew and began to think in her mind about the vision she saw the night her father returned. She kept thinking it over and over, hoping Andrew would get her message. After about ten times, she saw Andrew sit up straight and look directly at her. Once again, she thought about their father.

Andrew shook his head and tried to concentrate. Again, he had the same feeling that someone was talking to him, but it was from outside the house. As he thought about it again, he could suddenly see their house on the river, and Hannah was looking at him. She looked very sad. Then he heard her talking, not loud but in a whisper.

"Father returned to our house but as a spirit, not as himself. He was only here a short time, and then he was gone. He told me it was time to go, but I did not have time to get to him as I was not sure it was him. I think he is dead. He was likely killed in a battle."

Then she was gone. Andrew was horrified. Had he really heard this, or was he dreaming? He looked over at the group by the fire, and everyone looked fine. They had not seen or heard anything. He knew he could sometimes hear and see Hannah, but should he believe this terrible news? He must talk to Uncle William first. Hopefully, he would not think he was crazy.

When it was time to go to the barn to do the chores, Andrew followed his uncle quickly out to the barn. When they were feeding hay to the horses, he told him about the vision.

William was silent for a bit, and then he said, "I am not totally surprised. One of my sisters, when she was younger, could see people, so it may run in the family. I was worried as was your father that the battles were getting worse, and more men would be killed. The last time he was here, he asked me to care for your mother and you and your sister if anything happened. I will take a short trip to St. Davids to see what I can find out."

"I will go with you," Andrew answered quickly.

"No, you must stay here with the family to protect them, and you are of an age you can be taken into the militia, and that is the last thing your mother needs now. Do not speak of this to anyone else until I get back. I know that is a hard thing to do, but you must not tell anyone what you saw."

William told Elizabeth that night that he had to go for some supplies for winter in St. Davids and would be gone for at least five days. She was not happy with him, but she knew winter was coming, and she did have Andrew there to help.

William set off the next day with food and warm clothing as the weather could change at any moment. He hiked for two days, and by late that afternoon, he was on the edge of the small village of St. Davids. What he saw surprised and horrified him. Every house was gone. All that remained was the charred beams of the buildings. There were tents and lean-tos where residents had tried to make a shelter for themselves. A few animals were tied to half burnt trees, and dogs barked at anything that moved.

The Americans had been through here on their way elsewhere and had burnt the town. This was not what William had hoped to find. An elderly gentleman was just standing and staring into space in front of the flaps of a tent, so William approached and introduced himself. He asked several questions about when this had happened. The poor man was so shocked he could barely answer a simple question, so William gave him a few coins and went on his way.

Farther along the street, he came upon several women talking together. He again asked the same questions. This time, he was told how an American foraging party had clashed with some Canadian militia on patrol in July, and the American General was shot by the Canadians. A week later, as retaliation, the New York militia destroyed the thirty to forty houses in St. Davids. Several of our men from the village were killed as well as some of the militia.

William then asked, "Does anyone know the names of the soldiers killed at this spot?"

"They were buried at the cemetery by the other militia after the town was burned. I suppose the militia know who they were."

"Where would the militia be now?"

"We do not know where they have gone now. We are sorry. Did you know someone in the militia?"

"Yes," said William. "I suspect my brother was killed near here and about that time."

"This is a sad time for so many families. What is his name? Maybe someone left in the village might know him."

William gave the women David's name and then asked if he could camp in the village for the night before he traveled on. They were happy to let him stay and apologized for not being able to offer him better hospitality.

The next morning, William thanked the women he had talked to last night for allowing him to stay and packed his gear and began the journey toward the fort above the falls. It would take him another two or three days to get there, and hopefully, he would not encounter any trouble.

It was a sad journey as several small villages he came to had been destroyed by fire. He walked for another day and a half but found no militia at all or any more signs that they had been here fighting. He decided he had to turn back and return to the farm with no news for Sarah, just an ominous feeling.

*   *   *

Marilee awoke the next morning and felt as though she was fighting the war. She was exhausted. The dream she had last night revealed that Hannah's father had been killed during a skirmish at St. Davids. He was so close to home, and yet the inevitable happened. She knew that one of the graves in the historic cemetery had his name on a marker next to one with Sarah's name, and the dates coincided with the battle. Whether or not his body was there was really immaterial.

It was sad as Loyalist House, the family home of the Van Everys, still stood proudly along the river, even though the family had felt compelled to leave because of a war over land. She wondered if Hannah knew any of this. She suspected not as there had been no angry incidents, only sobbing. Either that or Hannah was becoming resigned to her plight. She decided to wait a bit to see what, if anything might happen in the attic before she tried to contact Hannah.

NOVEMBER

Marilee and Jeannie were sitting having coffee one morning talking about all the research they had completed over the past year and a half and what they would do with it now that they knew all about the Van Every family.

"Maybe we could put together a small book with photos of the area explaining the families' life," suggested Jeannie.

"That would be a nice thing for the guests to look at unless they were afraid of ghosts."

"Do we have any actual pictures of Hannah or anyone in the family?"

"Not that I know of," answered Marilee. I was thinking about a blog of some sort that ties into the B&B Web site. It might be good for advertising. I know it could turn off a segment of the tourists that were wary of ghosts in a house, but we sure have seen there are plenty of people who want to come here because of Hannah. We could use Hannah's name in the title and make it so it was alliteration, something catchy."

"You mean something like 'Hannah's Hopes and Dreams'?"

"Sure that's a good start. We could write about different family members, the hard life of the early settler, the foods they ate, all kinds of social activities that took place during that time."

"Marilee, I don't think your mind ever shuts off."

"Not often. That's probably why I have these crazy dreams all the time."

They continued with their plans for keeping Hannah in the forefront at Loyalist House and decided the one thing that was mandatory was a party for all their friends to let them know the final news about Hannah's family and about Peter. It would be a nice way to begin the Christmas season.

"Let's just invite the women we have pulled into our net," said Marilee. "Some of the men, husbands included, think we are a bit off at times, and they would just start discussing wine anyway. You and I can go over to the church one day and tell John personally about what we found. He would be interested, and we can take him a thank you gift. It's almost Christmas, so he wouldn't be embarrassed about accepting something."

"Great idea. Let's do it in the evening so the girls at the bakery can come. In fact, we could order some of their delicious shortbread for the party."

"For sure. Some wine and cheese and other Christmas appetizers, and later, coffee and cookies would be just perfect. Done! Plan complete. Now do you think we can convince the Loyalist House winery to supply the wine?"

They both laughed and figured out dates that would be good for a party. It was decided to have the party early in December before life became hectic with Christmas preparations. Jeannie would send out the invitations and make several appetizers, and Marilee would arrange for the rest of the food. This was the easiest party they had ever planned.

That night, Marilee was thinking about how she would present this information to their friends when she realized one part of the puzzle was still missing. She knew the house on the river was sold to a neighbor after the war, but she did not know what happened to Sarah and the children. Where did they go? Did they all stay at Williams? How did they all come to be buried in the one graveyard? She hoped she could find this out before the party.

She did not have to wait very long. The same night, she began to dream again of Hannah.

*   *   *

Hannah was still watching at the window for Peter. There had been some more movement on the river, but the boats carrying men continued past the dock both up and down the river. She had no idea where they were going. She had not been able to see across the distance to Andrew lately either, and this made her angry. Why was he ignoring her after she told him the information about their father? She decided to try once more tonight to see if he was paying any attention to her.

She was able to see into the cabin, and everyone was there except Uncle William. Andrew was looking out the window again.

Suddenly, Andrew jumped up and exclaimed, "Someone is coming. I think it may be Uncle William." He grabbed his gun and stood at the door just for safety reasons.

Outside, someone was deliberately stomping his boots and making noise so he would be heard. Soon, a familiar voice announced, "It is me, William. I am coming in the door."

The door opened, and in walked a cold and tired William. He looked at Andrew holding the gun and said, "I knew you would be ready for anything, and I did not want you to shoot me. I see you followed my suggestions."

Everyone ran to the door to welcome him back. Elizabeth was relieved he was home, and the children were very happy to see him again.

Andrew had mixed feelings. He was glad not to be the only one in charge anymore, but he was fearful of the news Uncle William might have about his father. He looked over at him and saw a look that said do not ask me now, wait until later.

His uncle was very tired, so after eating dinner, he retired for the night only saying that he would see Andrew for chores in the morning.

Andrew slept fitfully all night, and when morning finally came, he was the first one out to the barn. Uncle William arrived and immediately sat on some straw and motioned Andrew to join him.

"I did not really find out for sure if your father is dead or not. There was a skirmish at St. Davids where several Americans and some of our Canadian militia were killed. The Americans returned a few days later and burned the town in retaliation for killing their general. There is nothing left of the town, and there was no military there to give out any information. We do not know if David is alive and gone farther south with the militia. I do not want to tell your mother he is dead if he is not. What we will do is tell her about the burning of St. Davids and just wait until it is safe to go into Newark to find out information. The town is occupied now, but that might not last forever. I know this is hard for you not to know, but there is no other option."

Andrew agreed reluctantly but did not want to have his mother worry any more than she already did. That night, once again, he sat by the window looking toward the river. At one point, he could see Hannah watching him, almost asking him for information, but Andrew just shrugged his shoulders and turned away to be part of the family group by the fire.

Hannah was quite annoyed that Andrew was of no help to her at all. Her work now was to find Peter. She did not have time to worry about her father because Andrew did not want to. Why was he not taking some responsibility for the family? There was only so much she could do.

Since she was already down near the front door, she turned and went into the living room. The room had suddenly changed, and once again, there were pieces of furniture and odd items sitting on tables that she still did not recognize. She began by just walking around the room in a circle, but the more she thought about her frustration of not knowing where Peter was and her brother doing nothing, the more angry she became.

She walked faster and faster until she was literally flying about the room. Things began to fall off tables and fall on the floor.

Some pieces of china broke as it hit the hardwood, and a few small tables toppled over on their side, spilling books and ornaments. The room looked as though a tornado had gone through.

Hannah finally stopped circling and looked at the room. She had not meant to do this and was unable to pick anything up to replace it. She tried, but her hand just slipped right through the object. Now what would she do? Hannah flew back up to the attic and sat by the window and sobbed.

*   *   *

Marilee awoke in the morning feeling wonderful. She had slept through the night without waking. Then she recalled the dream she had. It was strange though, usually the dream woke her up but not this time. She remembered Hannah being angry, but she couldn't have destroyed anything as Marilee had not heard any loud noises in the night.

She put on her dressing gown and walked downstairs. As she walked through the hall, something on the floor in the living room caught her eye. When she walked into the room, she was horrified. The room was a mess. Furniture tipped over, figurines smashed, books open on the floor. This had to be Hannah's work. The only good thing was there were no guests in the house.

Phillip came in as she was putting things back in place. "What on earth happened in here?"

"I'm not sure. It must have happened in the night though I didn't hear anything. Did you hear any noise in the night?"

"Not really. If this is Hannah's work, then we are really going to have to do something like get that guy back and get rid of her. This is becoming ridiculous. You never know what is going to happen."

Marilee had never seen Phillip so angry. He didn't even wait for a response, just kept walking to the kitchen. She was going to have to seek out Hannah and try to get this whole mess straightened out soon before more things in the house were destroyed. She would call Jeannie today, and they try to come up with a plan.

Phillip didn't even stay around for breakfast. He just grabbed a coffee and went to his office in the Barn. After a few sips of coffee, he started to feel guilty. He should not have yelled at Marilee like that. It wasn't her fault as she had no control over Hannah. Except sometimes she did. He went back into the house and sat at the table with her, apologized, and they began to talk about how to change it.

Of course, there really was no sure answer, but Marilee convinced him they almost had everything figured out and would be able to make Hannah happy very soon. Just give her a few more weeks.

They changed the subject, talked about Christmas, where they were going to go this winter, and activities to plan when the kids came for the holidays. The second start to the day was much better than the first.

DECEMBER

This was the first night Marilee had wanted Hannah to be present either in her dreams or visible in the room. She hoped tonight Hannah would be angry or sad enough to want to talk and listen.

Tonight was the anniversary of the burning of the town of Newark in 1813. Hannah would surely see troops fleeing the area and possibly the glow of the fire. Marilee and Jeannie had all the information about her family and Peter ready to give to her. It was just a waiting game now.

Marilee did go to bed, but she found it hard to sleep in anticipation of visiting Hannah. She was reading when suddenly she looked up, and there was the filmy figure of the Hannah sitting on the chest across the room. She quietly put her book down and said, "Hello, Hannah. Do you want to go to the attic to talk? I have news for you."

The whitish-blue film began moving toward the door. Marilee followed up the stairs and sat in the rocking chair. She could see Hannah sitting by the window.

"What is happening tonight? I can see fire, and there are troops going in every direction?" asked Hannah in her husky voice.

Marilee then explained that the Americans had been occupying the town for the past seven months but had decided to pull out and go back across the river. When they left, they torched all the buildings in town. The townspeople had only a short warning so were unable to save most of their possessions.

It was a cold snowy night, and many were left in the street without shelter and only the clothes they were wearing. Those too sick to leave their home were carried out in their beds. One young girl was in her bare feet and stood on a silver platter her mother had saved. She suffered frostbite to her feet. It was a terrible time for everyone. By morning, only charred remains stood where the once first capital of Upper Canada had proudly been. As many of the men were away fighting, the victims were mostly women and children and the elderly.

"Were my parents in the town, or were they still with Uncle William?"

"No, Hannah, your parents were not in town, and your Uncle's home was safe. The Americans did not go that far west. They traveled across the river to Fort Niagara."

"Do you know if my father is dead?"

"I do know that, Hannah. I am sorry to tell you he probably was killed by the Americans during a skirmish in a small village not far from here called St. Davids. Your mother found out after the war was over. She could not bear the thought of coming back to this house without him and of course without you. She decided to sell this house and property to the neighbor to the north. Your uncle William helped her and asked her to live with them. He was given more land and ended up with over three hundred acres surrounding his cabin. Your brother helped him on the farm and stayed there after he married. Your sister stayed there too until she was married.

"We know all this because they are buried in a small cemetery on the edge of William's property. It has grave stones for both your mother and father and the other families related by marriage." Marilee stopped talking for a moment to see what Hannah would do or ask next.

Hannah was quiet for quite some time but remained a bright blue, so Marilee knew she was still there.

"Am I buried there?" she asked.

"We do not think so. We did not find your name on the gravestone, but as you were killed during the war, your parents may have buried you somewhere on the property. It was a troublesome time, and no one wanted to stray too far from home then.

"Is that why I am still in the house?"

"It may be the reason, but I think the real reason is you are waiting for Peter to return and have been watching for him all this time." Marilee decided to bring up the subject of Peter so Hannah would be ready for her answer.

"Do you know where Peter is, and do you know if he is coming back to me?"

Marilee took a deep breath and began the story she and Jeannie had discovered. "Peter went to your Uncle Samuel's farm as it was a safer distance from the fighting at first. The fighting then moved and was closer to the small farm. Samuel and his wife treated Peter as a son, and together they all moved quite a ways west to a safer spot. Peter helped them build a cabin and buildings for the farm, but he became restless and wanted to start out on his own. He said goodbye to Samuel and Hannah and moved closer to York which was a town across the lake. Did you know your uncle's wife was named Hannah?" Marilee had no idea how much Hannah knew about geography or her own family, so she tried to keep it as simple as possible.

"Yes, I knew that. I was named after her."

"Peter found a good job in York working in a store where people came to buy things they needed."

"Do you mean like a supply depot where my father would go to get seeds and things for the family?"

"Yes, it was much like that, but it also sold things you would need in your house as well. While he was working there, he met a girl at church. Her name was Agnes, and several years later, they were married. Peter knew you had been killed by the soldiers and was terribly sad for many years. He knew he could never come back and be in the same world as you. He wanted to have the life he dreamed you and he would have. Unfortunately, circumstances did not let that happen.

"Peter and Agnes moved to a large farm and raised eight children in the same community. You will be interested to know he named his second daughter Hannah. Maybe it was for both his mother and you, the two people who loved him enough to let him do what he wanted to do. I think you made such an impression on him, Hannah, that you helped shape his life. He became quite a respected man in his community, and his children all grew up to be wonderful people."

Again, it was silent in the room for quite a while.

Hannah then resumed her questions. "What will happen to me now? Peter is not coming back ever, and I think he is probably dead by now, but he is not a ghost here."

"Yes Peter is dead, and he is buried near where his farm was. He may be in heaven, or he may be a spirit elsewhere. That we do not know, and I do not think spirits can go to other's homes or attics to visit. We have to assume Peter will never come back here.

"You, however, do have some choices. You could decide to stay here and quietly live in the attic." Marilee decided to stress the quiet part. "Or you could decide to leave and go to the next world. There you may find your family and possibly Peter. You are the only one that can make the decision.

"If you stay here, we have to ask that you try not to get upset and destroy the rooms or scare the guests. You may wander about the house quietly when no one is here."

"I only do those things when I am angry at someone. I was angry at my brother the last time. Now that I know where they are and what happened to everyone, I will have no reason to be angry unless I forget. Do I have to decide right now?"

"No, Hannah, you may think about it as long as you want. I would just ask that when you have decided to, please tell me. We could still have chats if you like. Also, I am having a party next week to tell all our friends about your family story. It is a very interesting story, and they all know about your presence here at

Loyalist House. I just want you to know we will not be trying to find you that night like some of our guests did. You will be safe."

Marilee was getting tired, and she could see the blue light fading by the window as well. "I am tired and must go to bed now, but I will visit with you again, Hannah."

The light was very faint, but it looked like it was hiccoughing. Then Marilee heard the soft sobs as the light disappeared.

Marilee went back downstairs. Phillip was sound asleep and didn't stir as she slipped into bed. There were no dreams, no noises in the attic, or no sobbing sounds that night. The wind had been blowing from the south, but as the night went on, it changed direction; and by morning, there was a sharp north wind whipping the trees that protected Loyalist House.

EPILOGUE

Peter and Agnes were the third generation of Van Everys to settle in Upper Canada. In the Van Every family, Peter was the first born son of Samuel, even though in the story, he is adopted. It just seemed to add some interest to the story. Peter's grandfather was McGregory who came to Upper Canada as a refugee during the Revolutionary War. As a Loyalist, he fought to keep Canada under British rule and instilled in his family the importance of hard work and commitment.

In 1816, Peter and Agnes were married; and as a wedding present, Mr. Barry presented them with a hundred acres of land in Etobiocke Township that began at the lake and stretched north.

Peter built himself and Agnes the usual pioneer log house very much like the one he and Samuel had constructed in Ancaster. Later in 1838, he built a stone house which remained standing until 1952. He was obviously a good builder.

The Van Everys would have grown wheat, oats, rye, barley, corn, and peas, and over time, their wheat would have been traded with Europe, especially Britain. At that time, Britain was accepting under a preferential tariff all the flour Canada could send them. Many new flour mills were built on every river and stream to accommodate this need. This helped the growing community prosper, and many of the new farmers looked to people like Peter for leadership.

The Van Everys were proud of their Loyalists background, and many of their neighbors were as well. One such neighbor, the Goldthorpes, also Loyalists, lived close enough that the children all knew each other; and in the ensuing years, four Van Everys married four Goldthorpes. This, of course, was quite common because of great distances between villages.

Peter and Agnes Van Every had eight children between 1817 and 1836. Their first two children were girls named Margaret after Agnes's mother and the second Hannah. Could it be Peter was thinking of his Hannah, or was she named for Samuel's wife Hannah?

Peter's daughter Hannah married the neighbor boy John Goldthorpe, and they had seven children. Their sixth child, born in 1859, was named Augusta Jerusha and had a love of animals and stubbornly believed they should not be slaughtered for food. She was obviously well ahead of her time. While Augusta was in high school in Port Credit, she met a red-headed boy named James Thomson.

James at that time was a farm boy living with a family near Port Credit. He was one of seven boys, but as his father died at a young age, he was sent by his mother to a Port Credit family to live and work. Being a farmer, of course, meant slaughtering animals, but his new love for Augusta made him change his lifestyle, and he became first a barber then a bricklayer.

Augusta's parents were not thrilled with James as a suitor as they saw him as a chore boy with a quick temper. James was not only strong willed but also had an independent spirit, and he married Augusta when he was twenty-two and moved to Toronto where he worked in the contracting business. Eventually, he set out on his own and later partnered with his brother Thomas forming Thomson Brothers Limited.

Over time, James or J.B., as he was called, had opportunities to meet many important people needing contractors. One such family were members of the Eaton family. This led to

Thomson Brothers becoming the primary contractors for the T. Eaton Company. They would complete all the work for the Eaton stores across Canada as well as homes, cottages and churches built for the family.

The marriage between Augusta and James produced eight children in fourteen years—four girls and four boys. All the boys, when old enough, joined Thomson Brothers Limited. The oldest daughter, Amy, was the author's grandmother.

Many years later when the boys were grown and part of the company, J.B. was contacted by Connie Smythe about building a new arena in Toronto. It was the depression, and the job seemed impossible, but in five months, the job was completed. Maple Leaf Gardens opened in November 1931. It was not without controversy and creative scheduling, but Thomson Brothers kept their promise even during a depression.

From hardworking Loyalists protecting their homes while working the land to feed their families to entrepreneurs building edifices as part of an empire, the Van Every family had the grit and independent spirit needed to survive and help shape a nation. They were not the famous names recorded in Canadian history, but like so many others, they were the hardworking backbone of the nation.

WINE AND FOOD PAIRINGS

Chardonnay

Pesto dip with toasted French bread slices, apple slices, and raw
    almonds

Pesto dip: Using a homemade pesto or a purchased variety, mix
    with half a small container of spreadable cream cheese.
    Serve in a small bowl with spreading knife.

Apples: Slice apples with the skins on and sprinkle with powdered
    ascorbic acid or dip in orange juice to prevent browning.

Arrange all foods on a platter.

Riesling

Ginger chutney served with toasted French bread slices, candied
    walnuts, fresh apricots, and havarti cheese

Ginger chutney: Using homemade or purchased fruit chutney, add
    grated fresh ginger the day before. Serve in a bowl with
    spreading knife.

Candied walnuts: Dip walnuts in beaten egg white and then in course sugar or maple sugar and roast on pan for about ten to fifteen minutes at 375 Fahrenheit. Watch carefully as they will burn quickly. Serve in a bowl with small tongs or a spoon.

Arrange all foods on a platter.

Sauvignon Blanc

Lemon/grapefruit spread, toasted French bread slices, green apple slices or asparagus spears, and pine nuts

Lemon/grapefruit spread: Mix chopped peeled from one grapefruit with two tablespoons of lemon juice and half a small container of spreadable cream cheese or Greek yogurt. It should be a spreadable consistency.

Green apples slices: same as above.

Arrange all foods on a platter.

Pinot Noir

Mushroom caps with goat cheese, walnuts, and strawberries

Mushroom caps: Wipe mushrooms clean and remove stems. Set aside. Chop stems finely; chop two green onions finely. Sauté for several minutes in frying pan until liquid evaporates. Add about half a cup of fine bread crumbs and goat cheese to create a mixture of medium consistency. Spoon into mushroom caps. Place on baking sheet and place under broiler for two to four minutes. Serve hot. Small forks may be needed with serving plates.

Wash strawberries and serve with stems attached.

Serve strawberries on a separate platter from mushroom caps, and the walnuts in a bowl.

Merlot

Baked brie topped with caramelized onion and rosemary, fresh plums
Chop sweet onions and caramelize in a frying pan, adding either
small amount of brown sugar or maple syrup. Place brie
cheese round on an oven proof plate. Add onions and
chopped rosemary to top and place in 425 Fahrenheit oven
for about ten minutes to just warm up the cheese, not melt it.
Serve with toasted French bread slices and fresh yellow plums.

Cabernet Sauvignon

Assorted cheeses, dark sweet cherries, and lavender shortbread
Serve local old cheddar or gorgonzola cheese, dark sweet cherries
if in season on a platter. Using your favorite shortbread
recipe, add washed and patted dry lavender buds to the
dough. Bake as per recipe. This makes a lovely combination
of sharp and sweet to accompany the wine.

BIBLIOGRAPHY

1. Walter R. Bornemon, 1812 *The War That Forged a Nation*. New York: Harper-Collins, 2004.
2. Janet Carnochan, *History of Niagara*. Bellville, Ontario: Mika Publishing, 1973.
3. Dorothy Duncan, *Hoping for the Best, Preparing for the Worst: Everyday Life in Upper Canada, 1812-1814*.Toronto: Dundurn, 2012.
4. A. J. Langgath. *Union 1812: The Americans Who Fought the Second War of Independence*. New York: Simon & Schuster, 2006.
5. Richard Merritt, Nancy Butler, and Michael Power, editors, *The Capital Years: Niagara on the Lake 1792-1796*. Toronto: Dundurn Press and Niagara Historical Society, 1991.
6. John M. Macrae, *A Van Every Story*. Lakefield, Ontario, 1989.
7. Michael Power, Nancy Butler, *Slavery and Freedom in Niagara*. Niagara on the Lake: The Niagara Historical Society, 1993.